Where did he come from?

It was as though Cath had always known Doug. She could tell him things she'd never dare say to another person and he would understand. But when she questioned him about his past, his expression grew cloudy.

"We're supposed to be talking about you, not me," he said. Abruptly he reached over, touching the corner of her lips with one finger, a gesture that seemed too natural for Cath to be startled.

As their gazes met, energy crackled between them and Cath closed her eyes, suddenly frightened by the unexpected fire in Doug's look. The laughter had vanished completely from his eyes.

"I want you to know," Doug whispered solemnly, "I'm not exactly what I seem."

Dear Reader,

Although our culture is always changing, the desire to love and be loved is a constant in every woman's heart. Silhouette Romances reflect that desire, sweeping you away with books that will make you laugh and cry, poignant stories that will move you time and time again.

This year we're featuring Romances with a playful twist. Remember those fun-loving heroines who always manage to get themselves into tricky predicaments? You'll enjoy reading about their escapades in Silhouette Romances by Brittany Young, Debbie Macomber, Annette Broadrick and Rita Rainville.

We're also publishing Romances by many of your all-time favorites such as Ginna Gray, Dixie Browning, Laurie Paige and Joan Hohl. Your overwhelming reaction to these authors has served as a touchstone for us, and we're pleased to bring you more books with Silhouette's distinctive medley of charm, wit and—above all—*romance*. I hope you enjoy this book, and the many stories to come.

Sincerely,

Rosalind Noonan
Senior Editor
SILHOUETTE BOOKS

BARBARA BARTHOLOMEW
A Man of Character

Silhouette Romance

Published by Silhouette Books New York

America's Publisher of Contemporary Romance

For Martha Bartholomew
and in memory of A. J. Bartholomew

SILHOUETTE BOOKS
300 East 42nd St., New York, N.Y. 10017

Copyright © 1986 by Barbara Bartholomew

ISBN: 0-373-08428-5

First Silhouette Books printing April 1986

America's Publisher of Contemporary Romance

Printed in the U.S.A.

BARBARA BARTHOLOMEW

spent her childhood in western Oklahoma and thus has a feel for warm, country settings. A prolific author of adult and teen romances, Barbara is also an active member of the Romance Writers of America. When she's not writing, she enjoys spending time with her husband and three children in their Texas home.

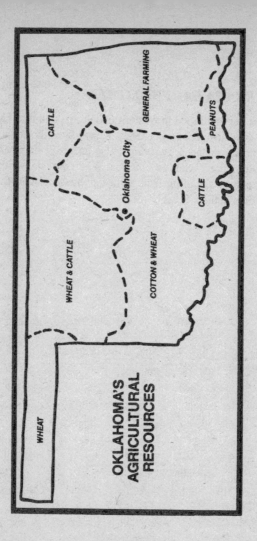

OKLAHOMA'S AGRICULTURAL RESOURCES

WHEAT

WHEAT & CATTLE

CATTLE

• Oklahoma City

GENERAL FARMING

COTTON & WHEAT

CATTLE

PEANUTS

Chapter One

Gran rushed into the house, slamming the door behind her. She looked indignant. "I can't even take a walk without being disturbed," she announced. "What's happened to us out here?"

Cathleen couldn't imagine why she was so upset, but knew it wasn't healthy. "Sit down, Gran, and let me get you something cool to drink."

It was only a few feet from the tiny living room into the kitchen. "I'll make ice tea," Cathleen said soothingly. "That'll taste good."

"For pity's sake, Cath. Don't talk to me as though I were senile."

Cath grinned. Gran was beginning to sound like herself again. "Sorry," she said. "But you are just recovering from a heart attack and shouldn't be out on a hot afternoon like this. And you certainly don't need to get excited about little things."

"Wasn't a little thing," Gran muttered in annoyance, but she did accept the tall glass of iced tea her granddaughter brought her, and sipped some before continuing. The angry lines vanished from her forehead, and she smoothed back her striking-looking white hair, looking somewhat more relaxed. "When you're my age, Cath, change gets to be hard to bear."

Cath grinned, settling herself with her own glass of tea in a chair where air from the evaporative cooler would blow across her with its gentle, moist breeze. "Nonsense, Granny, you're not old."

"Don't call me that abominable title," her grandmother snapped, then grinned sheepishly as she realized she was being teased. "Guess you're right. I'm barely in my seventies and my mother lived to be ninety, but this heart attack business..."

Her voice trailed off as she stared out the large front window to the pasture across the road where white-faced cattle lazily grazed in any shade they could find. One old cow had even found her way into the shallow water at the edge of the pond and stood halfway immersed, looking cool and comfortable. The familiar scene seemed to relax Gran. "I hate being trouble to everybody," she said, sounding a little less irritable.

"You're no trouble, Gran," Cath insisted, trying to push down the sick feeling that rose inside her at the thought of her own discarded plans. No matter how she felt, she wouldn't let her grandmother know just how much inconvenience having to come here for the summer had been.

A loud knock at the back door made her jump. "Who can that be?"

Gran sighed, then stretched a hand out to her. "I'm afraid you'd better ignore it, dear. Just pretend we're not here."

Bewildered, Cath stared at her grandmother. "Why should we want to do that?"

Gran leaned toward her. "That's why I was so upset. I'd just gone down to make sure the calves had plenty of water for this hot afternoon and was on my way back when I saw them coming." She spoke in a low voice, as though afraid of being overheard.

"Them?" Cath asked, her forehead wrinkling into a puzzled frown.

"You know, those people."

Another knock sounded, and Cath shook her head. "What people?"

"I forget you haven't been out here since it happened. Well, with the oil boom, we've had all kinds of strange people around here. You wouldn't believe how our quiet little community has changed."

Cath grinned. "It can't hurt for me to answer the door."

Gran frowned. "Don't be too sure of that. We are out here alone in the country, miles from everyone. Of course, I do have my old shotgun."

"It won't be necessary to shoot anyone." Cath leaned over to give her grandmother's elegant shoulder a pat. Still grinning, she headed for the door. When she opened it, she found that the caller had given up and was already headed back across the yard toward a dilapidated old van. A young, black-haired man stood by the van waiting for him.

The man who was walking away turned at the sound of the door opening, and his eyes met Cath's. When their gazes locked, she felt as though she'd just touched the electric fence that guarded the small herd of calves in the pasture back of the barn. Mind and body tingled.

He had the most unusual eyes she'd ever seen. Her own eyes were blue and so were his, but they were an unusual light blue, almost transparent, and fringed with dark lashes. He was tall and lean, looking as though he worked hard in the outdoors. His skin was weather-browned and his brown hair had sun-bleached streaks.

She realized she was staring. "Hello." Her voice came out as though unaccustomed to use.

He removed the battered straw hat that sat casually on his head. "Good afternoon. My friend and I are looking for work."

The voice was unexpected. His clothes were shabby, though clean. He looked like a wanderer, but his voice was cultured, educated.

She tried to smile, wondering why she was acting as if she'd lost her senses. She'd certainly met many more attractive men than this one—important men, doctors and teachers at the large hospital where she'd worked until recently. This one wasn't even handsome, though he had some unusual quality that she couldn't quite identify. "I'm sorry, we no longer manage a working farm. It belongs to my grandmother, but she retired years ago."

His smile made her wish she could befriend him. It was serious but engaging. She wondered how old he was—late twenties, she'd guess, or maybe early thirties.

His gesture swept the farm from the pasture and cattle to the growing cotton fields just to the northwest of the house. "Looks like a lot of work to me."

Up until this moment his friend had kept his distance, remaining in his position as an onlooker standing by the old van. But now he approached, perfect teeth flashing against dark skin. Anyone would have called this young man handsome, but somehow Cath's eyes strayed back to the other one.

He wasn't wearing a hat, but inclined his head slightly in a courteous gesture. "Pardon, *señorita*, my friend has forgotten his manners. I am Roberto Lopez and he is Douglas Boyd. We are seeking employment, even of a temporary nature."

"We'll do anything," the man called Douglas told her. "Slop hogs, feed chickens..."

Cath grinned wryly, beginning to feel more like herself. These two were as engaging a pair as she'd met in a long time. "I'm afraid we don't have hogs," she said. "And it's been at least ten years since Gran kept chickens." With one hand she gestured toward the chicken house down by the barn.

The two men looked at each other, and Cath couldn't help frowning slightly at what she saw in that exchange. Behind the charm she glimpsed fatigue and frustration. "Is it really that hard to find work?"

"*Si, señorita*," Roberto assured her. "We came here to work in the oil fields only to find the boom has passed by and there are no jobs. We need work to enable us to go elsewhere where there are jobs."

"Roberto!" his friend reprimanded, obviously embarrassed.

Roberto shrugged. "It is not a time for pride, my friend. Perhaps this young lady knows where we can find work."

Cath hesitated. She did have an idea, but she knew what her grandmother would say if she followed

through with it. "You might go talk to Whit Mc-
Michaels and tell him I sent you. He lives in the brick
house about two miles to the east." She pointed down
the dirt road. "He has lots of property of his own, and
he leases this farm from my grandmother. I heard him
say just the other day that he had more work than he
could handle. Maybe he could hire you."

"*Gracias, señorita*," Roberto smiled gratefully at
her.

His friend seemed less grateful. "This is kind of
you," he said awkwardly, as though he found accept-
ing favors difficult.

Cath nodded, then turned to go back inside. Gran
would have a fit if she knew about this. She just
wouldn't mention it. Probably Whit wouldn't hire
them, anyway, and that would be the last of it. She'd
never see the man with the light blue eyes again. What
had his friend called him? Douglas Boyd. A nice
name. She wondered if he was ever called Doug.

Once inside, she closed the door to protect the cool
house from the hot afternoon. She leaned thoughtfully against the door. What would Whit say if he
knew she'd been instantly attracted to a wandering
vagrant! Nature played funny tricks. Well, though she
could feel sympathetic to anyone in need, she certainly didn't admire healthy young men who got
themselves into such desperate situations. A little
planning and a lot of hard work would have pre-
vented it. She didn't feel any too sorry for them.

"What is it, Cath?" Gran called.

She went back into the living room. "Just some men
looking for work."

"Those men in the run-down old van that I saw
coming down the road?"

Cathleen frowned slightly. "That's who you were so frantic about?"

Her grandmother took on a defensive look. "It wasn't just because it was an old van. But it had an out-of-state license plate on it."

Cath realized she hadn't even noticed the plate. "You must have lots of people from out of state in the area because of the oil boom."

"We did. Most of them are gone now. Thank goodness."

Cathleen was tempted to argue. Gran had always been opinionated, but she'd never been unkind. It wasn't like her to take an immediate dislike to people just because they were strangers. But Gran's face looked thin and strained. She needed rest, not controversy.

Cath bent to give her a quick kiss on one softly wrinkled cheek. "I sent them on to Whit. Figured he could deal with them." She frowned again, remembering the man with the light blue eyes and the old-world courtesy of the other one. "Though they didn't seem so bad."

"Whit will send them packing. Maybe they'll go back where they came from."

"Maybe." Cath nodded absently. For a few minutes she'd lost the disappointed, empty feeling that had been too much with her lately, but it was back again. She told herself she had to make a deliberate effort to shake it off. The last thing she wanted was for Gran to get it into her mind that her granddaughter's presence here was a sacrifice.

"It's about time I started thinking about making dinner." She knew she sounded a whole lot more cheerful than she felt. "What do you feel in the mood for?"

"Oh, anything will do for me." Gran's voice was thin and remote. "I'm not that hungry."

"But you will be by suppertime." Cathleen tried to sound more assured than she felt. Gran didn't want to eat these days. Always thin, she was still losing weight. It was one of Cathleen's goals for the summer to get her grandmother back on a healthy diet. "Why don't I get out the grill and charcoal a couple of those steaks you have in the freezer? I'll make a salad and get some of those green beans you canned last year."

"That'll be lovely, dear." Obviously Gran was barely listening. "I do wish all these people would go away and leave us the way we were. I used to never even lock the door and now I'm afraid not to. Did you know Peggy Martin's house was broken into just last week?"

Cath nodded. "You mentioned it."

Gran shook her head. "It was while Peggy was in town seeing the doctor last Monday morning. She was getting her blood pressure checked. Can you imagine anyone mean enough to break into someone's house while she's at the doctor's?"

Cath eyed her grandmother thoughtfully. This wasn't the first time the subject had come up. Gran seemed to be dwelling on the problems associated with the sudden growth of the community since the oil boom. This fear was getting in the way of her full recovery.

"I don't suppose they knew Mrs. Martin was ill," she answered slowly, wishing there were something more comforting to say.

"Wouldn't care if they did. The police said the thief was probably watching the house and waiting for her to leave."

Cathleen decided it was time to change the subject. "We've got to get you out visiting your friends again. And you've always loved that crafts club that you and Mrs. Martin attend together. How about going this week?"

"Perhaps. If I feel well enough. I just don't seem to want to leave the farm these days."

"Go for my sake, then. I'll go along this first time. It'd be fun to get out and see some people." It was meant only as a pretext to get Gran going again, but it had an undesired effect.

Her grandmother glanced up with a worried look. "Oh dear! Poor Cath, stuck way out here in the country with your old grandmother. I'm such a nuisance to everyone."

It was so unlike Gran that for a minute Cath was startled. She couldn't help remembering what Gran had been like during summer visits: fun, independent, always active. This thin, sad woman hardly seemed like her grandmother. "Gran, I'm glad to be here with you."

Gran's smile was bitter. "How can that be? How can a girl in her twenties like sitting around with a sick old woman? And it's not just you. Your parents have taken so much trouble. Your mother stayed for weeks when I was so sick. I'm disturbing everyone, messing up their lives...."

Involuntarily, Cath's mind turned to her own disarranged plans. After years of working toward a goal, it had been within sight this summer, and she'd had to put it aside because of Gran. Never would she let her grandmother guess that.

"It's just because you've been sick that you're talking this way, Gran. You know I've always loved spending summers with you. Didn't I do it often enough when I was a kid?"

Again her grandmother smiled, this time less cynically. "Children always love visiting a farm, but now that you're grown-up and a nurse, you've got your own things to do, your own friends to keep you company. It's different now."

"And I still love visiting you." That was true, but Cath couldn't help feeling guilty that Gran was basically right. She'd planned to spend her summer in Mexico City, not on a small farm in western Oklahoma.

She got to her feet. No sense sitting here debating the matter anyway. It would take more than words to get Gran going again. It would take time, good company, a reminder of the fact that she still had a purpose in her life even if she was over seventy. Maybe this was the right place for Cath to be after all. Hadn't she carefully considered this decision to go to Mexico? But she felt that although others could take her place there, nobody else could replace Cathleen Carroll where her grandmother was concerned. However, she was only human and she still had moments of feeling rebellious. She'd waited years for the opportunity that she'd had to give up.

A booming knock sounded at the door, making them both jump.

"Do you suppose those men are back again?" Gran whispered as though afraid they might hear. "Maybe they only came before to size us up and they're back to rob us."

Cath touched her shoulder. "I'm sure it's not them." She ran to peer out the window. "It's Whit's pickup," she reported.

Once, Gran would have rushed to the door herself to greet her neighbor, but this time she just called. "Well, go see what he wants."

"Hi, Whit," Cath said as she greeted the tall, strongly built farmer whom she'd known for years. But then she stopped in surprise when she saw he was not alone. Her visitors of a few minutes before stood at his side.

Whit grinned with his usual friendliness. "Hi, Cath," he said. "Was just about to do some employing and thought I'd better check it out with Mrs. Price first." He turned to indicate the two men accompanying him. "Meet Roberto Lopez and Douglas Boyd, Cath. Cathleen Carroll," he finished the introduction.

"We've met," Cath told him. "Didn't they tell you I sent them over to your place?"

"We didn't get that far, Miss Carroll." Lopez smiled charmingly. "We barely introduced ourselves to Mr. McMichaels and asked about work when he insisted we come over here."

Whit loomed larger than either of the strangers—big, weather-bronzed and comfortingly familiar. He laughed. "I tell you I've just been so far behind that I jumped at the chance to get a couple of willing workers. Now, I warn you it's dirty work. Right now I need cotton choppers, and if you've never done that before, you'd best know right now that it gets hot, dusty and pretty miserable out there if you're not used to field work.''

Roberto Lopez smiled again. "I have worked with cotton before," he said with just a trace of a Spanish accent. "I grew up in the Rio Grande Valley, where we also raised cotton.''

Whit looked interested. "They do a lot of irrigating down there, don't they?''

Roberto nodded. "That's right.''

"Wish we could do more." Whit shook his head. "I'm piping in some water from a pond to my feed, but I just can't manage irrigating the cotton. Haven't needed it so much this year, though, since we've had plenty of rain." His gaze moved to the other man, Douglas Boyd. "How about you? You experienced working with cotton?''

Boyd looked a little dazed, shaking his head slowly. "No, but I'll do my best." He looked at his friend. "Roberto and I are willing to try anything.''

Cath frowned. He acted a little strange, this Douglas Boyd, as though he were in unfamiliar territory and didn't know the ground rules. She'd be almost willing to swear that in most circumstances he was very self-confident and capable. But something had shaken his assurance. The frown turned into a grin as she realized she was making a lot of assumptions based on two very brief meetings.

"Cotton chopping isn't that complicated." She found herself wanting to help. "I can even do it." She looked at Whit. "In fact, I'll offer my services if you're really short of help. Gran is well enough that she doesn't need me hanging around all the time. She'd probably be glad to get rid of me now and then.''

"Now, that's coming up in the world, having a registered nurse working in my fields. I'll sure take you up on that," her neighbor assured her. "If you can just get your grandmother to meet my new help here... You'll actually be working on Mrs. Price's land," he explained to the two men. "I lease it from her, but I know from experience that she's going to insist on passing approval on anybody that's going to be around here."

Once, that would have been only a formality. Cath found herself lowering her voice slightly. "Since she's been ill, Gran has been a little upset by strangers."

Whit was almost as familiar with the house as she, so he went past her and led the way. Roberto walked at his side, leaving Douglas Boyd to follow with Cathleen.

"Did you grow up in the country?" she asked, trying to make conversation. Something about this man made her uneasy; she wasn't sure what it was.

He smiled, a grave, serious smile that left her feeling flooded with unexpected sunlight. "I'm a real novice to country life. I'll probably do everything wrong."

So that was why he'd seemed so out of place. And yet it had seemed something more.

"I grew up in Oklahoma City myself, but I've always spent summers with Gran, so I can help show you the ropes."

"Thanks. Did Mr. McMichaels say you're a nurse?"

"That's right. I've taken a leave of absence for the summer to look after my grandmother. She had a heart attack last spring."

He nodded.

"What about you? What do you do?" It was only after she'd asked that she realized she was being tactless. A man like this, a wanderer looking for any work he could find, wouldn't know how to respond to such a question.

"I've been in school," he responded, seeming more relaxed. "In Waco and then—" He stopped suddenly, then grinned weakly. "Guess there are a lot of dropout students in this world."

Obviously he didn't want to talk any more about himself. He had suddenly realized he'd said more than he'd intended. He was a puzzle, Cath decided. An apparently cultured, well-educated man brought to this subsistence level of living. What road had led him here?

Chapter Two

By the time Cath and Douglas Boyd joined the other two in the living room, Gran was already regarding her visitors with open suspicion. She remained silent while Whit made the introductions and explained why he'd brought the two men by.

Her attention focused on Douglas. "You aren't from around here." It was an accusation.

He smiled, not seeming at all disconcerted by her attitude. "No ma'am," he said. "Fact is, I'm a Yankee."

"Oklahoma was not a part of the old South, young man, but I am a Southerner by birth. I was born in Kentucky."

"A lovely state."

"I wouldn't know. I was brought here when I was only a year old." She turned to the other man. "You look foreign."

Cath flinched. It wasn't like Gran to sound prejudiced, but she could be direct. "Mr. Lopez said he's from south Texas," she said hastily.

"That is correct," Roberto agreed. "However, my parents brought me to Texas from Mexico when I was ten. My roots are there, and we speak both Spanish and English in our home."

Cath couldn't help feeling a little envious. She'd been planning on spending the summer working on a skill that he'd picked up naturally. Maybe she could get him to give her lessons.

Gran wasn't interested in these details. "We've been getting lots of strangers in here. People hoping to get rich off the oil without even having to work."

Douglas smiled, and Cath watched her grandmother respond to the warmth that had had such a powerful effect on her. "Roberto and I came here hoping for jobs."

Gran eyed him sharply. "Wasn't there any work where you were?"

Roberto was the first to answer. "Things are difficult in the valley right now," he explained. "Unemployment is very high. It is not that I didn't wish to work, Mrs. Price." He was quietly dignified, refusing to bend in spite of the fact that he was here as a supplicant.

"Things aren't too good in the industrial north, either," Douglas added.

Cath frowned. From what he said, it seemed he came from the North, but only minutes before, he'd told her of his attendance at a school in Texas. Something didn't add up here.

Gran looked at Whit. "I'm sure these are fine young men, but I'd prefer you hired someone local to work on my property."

Whit looked taken aback. Obviously he hadn't expected opposition. "Everyone's busy getting their own work done, Mrs. Price. Nobody's looking for cotton-chopping jobs. I even hired Cath here; that shows how desperate I am." He grinned, his usual sense of humor back in force.

"I don't want to do all the work myself, Gran." Cath wondered why she was pleading for two men she didn't even know. Maybe just because it wasn't fair to turn them away only because they were strangers. Still, she could understand her grandmother's fears. Crime had skyrocketed in the community since the oil-field workers had come.

Gran glanced from Whit to Cathleen, a worried look on her face. She seemed to be waiting for something.

"Mrs. Price, we may be the world's worst cotton choppers, but we'll do our best." It was Douglas speaking, leaning down toward the woman with a concern that seemed genuine. Cath found herself watching him closely. He wasn't just putting on that manner; he liked her grandmother. She was almost sure of it. Not everyone had the patience or insight to deal this way with an elderly, sick woman.

"Speak for yourself," Roberto addressed his friend teasingly. "I'll have you know, Doug, that I have always been considered the best cotton chopper in my entire family."

Whit came to their defense. "It's not like I'm hiring 'em permanently, Mrs. Price. It'll only be a couple of weeks and we'll have the work laid by."

Mrs. Price rubbed at her forehead as though it ached. Cath stepped closer. Gran shouldn't be having to bother with this when she was feeling so ill, and yet she would have been even more upset if Whit had hired someone to work on her property without consulting her. This farm had been in her family her entire life. It was almost an extension of her. Suddenly she waved her hand as if dismissing them. "Whatever Cathleen says. I'll let her decide for us."

Cath didn't like having the responsibility dumped on her. Her instincts told her that the kind thing was to offer the men the work. And yet Gran's fears were not totally unrealistic. She was hardly conscious that she shook her head. Hiring strangers probably didn't make a whole lot of sense. But she couldn't just keep batting the decision back and forth as though it were a table tennis ball. "What do you think, Whit?"

"I really need the workers. And these guys seem to have plenty of muscle."

Cath swallowed, too conscious of the muscular arm of the man closest to her. He was only inches from her, warm and real. It would be easier for her if he went away. But still . . . "I don't see why we can't give it a try."

"Great!" Roberto Lopez smiled broadly at her. Douglas Boyd stuck out a hand, and she had no choice but to shake it.

"Thanks very much, Miss Carroll," He said. "You won't regret it."

"You can start first thing in the morning," Whit told them. "Just show up bright and early. I'm certain Cath will be out there to help you." He grinned challengingly at her, and she was sure he didn't think she would actually go through with it.

"I'll be there," she assured him.

After saying goodbye to Mrs. Price, they headed toward the door. "Where will you guys be staying?" Whit asked his new employees casually.

"We haven't found a place yet," Douglas answered quickly.

"It can be rough. Not much around here but a couple of motels up to town, and they run expensive."

"Not what we're looking for," Roberto said. "But we'll find something."

"Hope so." Whit looked doubtful.

Cath couldn't help wondering if they lived in that old van. She'd heard of people who lived in cars, tents, anything available. Surely not! She dismissed the thought.

Douglas Boyd turned to her. "We'll be seeing you in the morning, then, Miss Carroll."

"You sure will." She cast a defiant glance at Whit. "But you might as well call me Cath if we're going to be working together. It's short for Cathleen."

"Cathleen suits you better. It's a lovely name."

Cath was uncomfortable. What an odd thing for a man like him to say. A man like him . . . What was he like?

"I'll pack a lunch," she offered impulsively. "Part of your payment for working."

As they walked away, she wondered why she'd promised them a meal. Then she realized: somehow she was afraid they were hungry.

It was a disconcerting feeling. Most of the people she knew were far from rich. She'd had to work her own way through nursing school. But she'd never before met anyone who actually was suffering from want of food.

Cath headed back to the living room, but when she got there she found her grandmother had fallen asleep in her chair. She stared thoughtfully at her. People had always said she looked like Gran, with her delicate but decisive features and slender, long-limbed form. She grinned at the thought. Dad always said they looked like thoroughbreds. She wasn't sure she liked being compared to a horse, and when she'd said so, he'd told her he meant they combined elegance with sensitivity. Maybe that was the trouble now. Gran was too sensitive. She seemed to know that Cath didn't want to be here, no matter how she tried to disguise that fact.

Suddenly, Gran's eyes, still as blue as the ocean, opened. "Cath?" She frowned. "I wasn't asleep, only resting."

Cath grinned. "Sure, Gran." Gran smiled back, both of them enjoying the joke. It was the first moment they'd really shared this summer.

"Come on, Gran. It really is getting close to suppertime now, and you can help me get it ready."

"I'd like that." Gran got up, leading the way into the sunny kitchen that had been decorated in yellow ever since Cath could remember. "But it's too late to thaw steaks."

"We could if we put them in the microwave."

"If I had a microwave." Gran grinned. "Your mom tried to get me one of those gadgets, but I told her the old ways were good enough for me."

Cath tried to put on a severe expression. "Then I presume we're going to cook our meal over that old kerosene stove you've got stored away in the cellar."

Gran laughed. "I'm not quite that old-fashioned. We can use the gas range. But since it's too late for the steaks, why not let me plan the menu?"

Cath looked thoughtfully at her grandmother. Had everyone, including herself, fallen a little too much into the habit of thinking and planning for Gran since she'd gotten sick?

"Just don't forget I'm a nurse and I can't let you eat anything that's not nutritious."

Gran sighed. "I don't know if it's nutritious or not, but it's what I grew up on. I'm hungry for corn bread and buttermilk, fresh sliced tomatoes and some of those green beans you mentioned before. A homemade custard with lots of eggs and fresh milk would be a nice change for dessert." She looked defiantly at her granddaughter.

"Doesn't sound like anything that would kill you." Cath grinned. "If you'll give me directions, I'll prepare it."

"I'll let you make everything else, but I'm putting the corn bread together myself. Nobody can make it like I do."

"That's a deal."

They laughed and talked as they prepared the simple meal her grandmother had planned. It was more like old times than any they'd spent together since Gran's illness.

When her alarm went off the next morning, Cath was tempted to silence it and go back to sleep. It was so early it was still dark outside. But then she remembered the snide tone that had been in Whit's voice when he kidded her about working in the field, and she rolled out of bed. She and Whit had been summertime friends since she was a little girl, and his favorite pastime was teasing her. She'd never hear the last of it if she didn't at least show up this morning.

And she'd promised the hands lunch. Drat! Why hadn't she thought about that last night? Now she'd have to hurry to get something together. If Gran didn't feel the way she did, she could have just brought the men back to the house to eat, but under the circumstances that might not be wise.

She showered hastily, trying to wake up, then yawned as she dressed in her oldest blue jeans and a long-sleeved shirt that would protect her fair skin from the sun. She dug through the utility closet, hoping to find an old straw hat, but she finally had to settle for one of the bonnets that Gran made herself, knowing that she'd look like something out of *Little House on the Prairie*. But even that was preferable to ending up with a toasted face. She also found a pair of gardening gloves. She'd never chopped weeds from cotton before, but she'd hoed Gran's garden plenty of times and knew that blisters were another hazard.

She got out the small ice chest that she'd bought for travel and heaped in as many ice cubes as the refrigerator freezer contained. Then she put in sandwiches made with thick slices of country ham. She added a vine-ripened tomato and some lettuce to be put in the sandwiches. She selected pieces of fruit from the bowl Gran always kept on the table: a couple of bananas and several luscious-looking peaches. She thought about making iced tea, but realized she'd already taken all the ice. She looked through the refrigerator for something to drink and finally settled on a container of grape juice. At least it was cold. She put it in the ice chest and hoped that was enough food. Nothing else would fit. She put paper plates, cups, napkins and a generous amount of homemade peanut butter cookies into a paper sack.

It was beginning to grow light outside. How come morning came so early in the summer? Hurriedly, she fixed herself a large bowl of cereal and a cup of instant coffee. After she ate, she wrote a note for her grandmother, reminding her that she'd be in the nearby field. Grabbing up her supplies, she headed outside.

She was beginning to really wake up, and the early-morning air felt soft and moist. Birds were singing the first notes of dawn, and she could hear the bawl of a calf in the pasture back of the barn. She couldn't help wondering why she hadn't gotten up at this time of day before. She was reminded of the old song from the musical *Oklahoma*: "Oh, What a Beautiful Morning!"

Whit's pickup was parked down by the barn, and she could see him moving about, feeding the calves. These days the livestock all belonged to him, though Gran took a proprietary interest in their welfare. She started to walk down to join him, then decided 'it would be more fun if she was already at work in the field when he arrived. That way she could tease him about getting to work late.

She got a hoe out of the shed and, loaded down with the little ice chest, the paper sack and her hoe, hiked across to the cotton field east of the house.

The battered van was already parked beside the field. Nobody could accuse Douglas and Roberto of being reluctant to get to work. It wasn't even fully light yet. She hoped they weren't out there chopping down cotton plants, mistaking them for weeds.

They were both hard at work, concentrating intensely as they moved down the rows between cotton plants. She felt a little shy about approaching them, wishing Whit were here to help ease the meeting.

"Hi, guys," she called as she came up. "Hard at work already, I see."

Roberto was farther away, apparently having accomplished more on his rows. Douglas glanced up, seeming to be startled out of deep meditation.

"Good morning, Cathleen. I didn't expect to see you here so early."

Funny how everyone took her to be a cream puff. She decided not to be offended. "I probably wouldn't have made it if the thought of how Whit would tease me hadn't spurred me on."

His intense eyes studied her. "The two of you are old friends?"

"Old enemies is more like it. I've always spent summers here and he's always given me a hard time. He'd make rude comments about how girls couldn't do this or that as well as boys could. So, of course I had to show him."

"And you're still showing him?"

Cath grinned. "I suppose so."

"*Buenos dias*, Miss Carroll," Roberto called from halfway up the field.

"It's Cath," she called back as a reminder. "How's it going?"

"Fine! Lots of weeds."

As if reminded, his friend resumed his work. "Don't suppose we're being paid for standing around."

"Guess not." Cath put her small stock of food in the shade of the scrubby little mesquite tree that stood near the fence and prepared to go to work. She took the two rows next to Douglas and began hacking at a large weed. Her hoe turned out to be so dull that the work was made doubly hard.

"Mr. McMichaels left a file when he brought the hoes for us," Douglas suggested. "If you'd like to sharpen your hoe."

Gratefully, she did as he suggested, wincing at the abrasive sound of file against hoe, but when she went back to work, chopping went more easily.

Douglas chopped some of the weeds in her row so that she could catch up with him. "It'll be more interesting if we can talk to each other," he explained somewhat defensively.

"Thanks," she said a little breathlessly. Working as a nurse in a large hospital was hard work, but not in this way. She was finding out that she wasn't in quite as good condition as she'd believed. She glanced at him, then frowned. "Don't you know you ought to be wearing gloves? You'll have blisters all over your hands." Her next thought was that the remark might have been tactless. She looked ahead to where Roberto was working. No gloves there either. Was it that they couldn't afford something as inexpensive as work gloves? "But maybe your hands are tougher than mine."

"I hope so." His smile this time lit his eyes with amusement. "Yours are certainly prettier."

His were browned and strong-looking, but they seemed well cared for, considering he was a man accustomed to outdoor work. She wondered if he was one of the many laid off from industries in the North. He hadn't pretended to a background in farm work.

"Gran always has some old gloves around from when Dad or my uncles were here helping with the garden. I'll find a pair for you."

"Oh, don't bother. I'll buy some the first chance I get."

So he was too proud to accept help. How silly!

They worked in busy silence for several minutes. The sun was fully up now, a blazing ball of heat on the horizon. After a few more minutes had passed, Whit drove up. He got out and went over to pick up a hoe to begin sharpening it.

"Don't tell me the boss is going to condescend to work with us," Cath called.

"Just for today," he shouted back. "Tomorrow I'll have to get back to work on the tractor."

She couldn't help wondering if he had come out today just so he could get a good look at how his new hands were working out. It wasn't a very big risk, after all, to trust them with inexpensive equipment like a couple of hoes. But it'd take a little more faith to turn them loose on one of his big tractors or have them look after valuable cattle.

Somehow she felt they could be trusted. She hoped Whit would eventually let them have a chance at more responsible chores, though probably they would have moved on by then. Men like them didn't stick around long.

Once Whit started to work on his rows, she intensified her own chopping, determined not to give him a chance to tease her about her puny efforts. But in spite of the fact that Douglas was still assisting with her weeds as well as keeping up his own rows, Whit soon pulled abreast of them.

"You city girls just don't know how to do this kind of thing," he teased, straight-faced.

"I got here before you did. You can't say I don't know how to get up early."

"Early! Why girl, it must have been close to six when you came out of the house."

Cath had always thought of 6 A.M. as being a very early hour. "What time did you get here?" she asked Douglas.

"About dawn."

She frowned at him. Did he seem more withdrawn now that Whit had come up?

"But she's been working really hard since she got here, Mr. McMichaels."

"Nobody calls me Mr. McMichaels." Whit sounded insulted. "And you don't have to cover up for Cath, Douglas. I've noticed you giving her a little assist there on the side. But you know how girls are, just don't quite have the muscle to keep up with us."

Douglas glanced uneasily at them, obviously wondering if he was going to be caught in the midst of a fight. Cath grinned. He'd have to learn that she and Whit fought like cats and dogs, or like brother and sister!

"You've gone soft sitting up in the air-conditioned cab of that tractor of yours," she said accusingly. "You'll be lucky if you can keep up with me after I've had a few days to get into practise."

"Come on, Cath! Admit it. You'll never last out the day."

"Is that a dare?"

"Not that. It's a sure thing. Once the sun gets hot, you'll begin to melt like iced sherbet next to a hot stove. You're just like my wife. You were designed for the luxurious life."

"You're married, then, Whit?" Douglas asked, trying to strike up a conversation.

"Was." Whit was overly casual, Cath knew, to hide deep feelings. He'd been crushed when his wife of over five years had packed and left him with virtually no warning. "Angie decided the farm life wasn't for her and went back home to her folks. She's working in Dallas now and planning on getting a divorce."

"Oh, sorry."

"Yep, me, too, but I guess I'll adjust."

Douglas nodded. "It can be rough. But maybe you can still work things out."

Whit shook his head. "Not likely. Anyhow, it's Angie's turn to try to fix things up. She's the one who left me."

"Still, it's not always that simple."

Whit took on a stubborn look. "It is for me. She left me, and that's all there is to it."

Cath didn't like this turn in the conversation. Her old friend came across as tough-skinned, but she knew that in reality he was easily hurt. The collapse of his marriage had been the hardest blow of his life.

Whit didn't seem to want to talk anymore. With unaccustomed silence, he began to concentrate on his work, soon pulling ahead of his less experienced co-workers.

Douglas watched Whit retreating for only an instant then returned to work. "Guess we'd better get going or the boss will fire us," he said, smiling briefly at her.

The blue eyes seemed to look right through her. She wondered what he was thinking.

Chapter Three

Cath couldn't guess that Douglas Boyd's thoughts were, for once in his life, quite uncomplicated. He was thinking that the blisters on his palms burned, that the sun was warm and that Cathleen Carroll was a very pretty girl. Not a girl really; she was probably no more than four or five years younger than he. And he was feeling every day of his twenty-nine years lately.

Cathleen was a complication he hadn't expected. Why was it that when life was just at its most confusing point, something else came along to mix it up further? He glanced at her, bent over her hoe. Even with that funny-looking bonnet tied at her chin, she was a lovely girl with fair skin only slightly tanned to a honey color, enormous blue eyes and hair the shade of molten gold. Her smile was sweet and shy. She was just the kind of woman who would have attracted him if circumstances had been different. But the way things were, it was best to keep a distance between them. He almost laughed when he realized his own presumption. Cathleen Carroll wasn't likely to waste her time thinking about him, not when she thought he was a wanderer looking for a chance employment, living in a van—not that she knew about that.

It wouldn't change things if she knew who he really was, what he actually did. No, it would definitely be better if he kept his mind from straying to her as much as possible.

He didn't say anything else to her as they worked their rows to the end of the field and then chose two more each to start back. "You seem to be taking to this real well," she said, sounding a little breathless.

He laughed mirthlessly. "I'm glad for the job," he said. "I don't want to fool around and lose it."

"Whit doesn't expect you to kill yourself."

"He does expect me to do my best. And obviously my best isn't up to his standard or Roberto's."

She grinned, preparing to challenge his reasoning. "This is some kind of macho thing, then. You've got to keep with with them."

It annoyed him that she was so right. It should be enough just to know he was doing the best he could; he wasn't in competition with the other two, and yet he wanted to do as well or even better.

"Don't be so hard on yourself," she advised.

They chatted a little more comfortably as they worked their way back to the starting point, talking about the farm, the work, the day. He found himself wanting to know more about her.

"You're a nurse? That's why you came out to look after your grandmother?"

"That's part of it. I'd planned to take a leave of absence this summer, but my parents called and asked me to come look after Gran. Dad had stayed out here as long as his job allowed, and then Mom stayed on even after that. Dad said Mom was getting so worn down that he was worried about her, but I think it was partly just that he missed her so much. Gran and I have always been close, so I was the logical one to come."

"Still, it must have been hard to interrupt your vacation."

"It wasn't exactly a vacation, but yes, it was hard. Don't say anything to Gran, though. She'd feel badly if she knew. She's already worrying that she's bothering everyone."

"You're lucky to have a family like that," he told her, feeling a little envious. "People who care about each other."

"I suppose." She didn't sound too sure, and he guessed the interrupted vacation plans had been a bigger disappointment than she'd admitted. He could understand that. Nurses didn't make that much money. She'd probably saved a long time for a cruise or a fabulous trip with her friends. Anyone would find something like that hard to give up.

"How about you? What's your grandmother like?"

The question startled him. "I always called her 'Grandmother.'"

She grinned again. "How unusual."

He couldn't help matching the grin. "I noticed how you called yours 'Gran.' Sounded so nice and informal, and you seemed to be such friends."

"Sure. We've always been pals. She was my last refuge even when Mom and Dad were mad at me. Isn't your grandmother like that?"

"Not really." Inadvertently, his mind pictured the stiff-backed lady who was his grandmother. She was younger than Cathleen's gran and, fashionable and chic, she looked younger, too. But he couldn't imagine sitting around chatting with her. And the last time he'd seen her, she'd been very angry with him. He had failed to live up to the expectations she'd cherished for the only Boyd grandson. "No, my grandmother's different from yours."

They weren't that many yards behind Whit and Roberto by the time they neared the end, and the other two helped them finish their rows so that they could all have a drink from the thermos of ice water Whit had furnished. They then took turns sharpening their hoes.

"I've got to take a break and go check on Gran," Cathleen told them, pushing back her bonnet to smooth back moist, tumbled curls.

"Excuses, excuses!" Whit grinned. "Already taking off on me."

"I'll be right back." She made a face at him, then strode off toward the house, her long, slender legs moving quickly across the rows. Douglas watched her go. He liked to observe the motion of her lithe form, crossing the field with fluid gracefulness. He'd never known anyone like her before.

Watch out, he warned himself, suddenly aware what he was thinking. You can't afford this. Not now.

He looked around, conscious that the other two men had noticed he was eyeing her. "*Muy bonita*," Roberto observed.

"Very," Douglas agreed a little sheepishly, taking his turn with the file.

"I don't know what that means," Whit drawled, "but if you're saying something insulting about Cath..."

"Roberto was just observing how pretty she is," Douglas explained hastily.

"She's real good looking," Whit agreed, "and nice, too. Not many girls these days would take off to come stay with their grandmas."

Douglas found himself wondering what the relationship between the two was. Whit had said he was getting divorced. Maybe his future plans included Cathleen. The thought was painful. How could he feel jealous about a woman he'd only just met? But there was no denying the instant attraction he'd felt. It was as though he'd recognized her, been looking for her all his life. Why did this have to happen now when he couldn't do anything about it?

"I've got to take off a few minutes myself," Whit told them. "Need to check and see if the calves have enough water."

Thoughtfully, Douglas watched him go. They hadn't been working that long. Surely he'd checked his calves before he started. Maybe he'd only gone to join Cathleen and spend a little time with her alone.

"I believe he wants to see how we work when he isn't present." Roberto's voice penetrated his thoughts. "So perhaps we'd better get on with it."

Douglas nodded. He got another drink of water and started back toward the cotton rows.

"Are you finding this very difficult? You're not accustomed to working like this."

Douglas shrugged. "It's not any harder than working on a drilling rig."

Roberto nodded. "And it is work. It will buy food for a few days."

Douglas looked curiously at his friend. He and Roberto had met only a few weeks ago when they'd accidentally found themselves working together, but he already felt an involvement with the younger man's problems. For him this was only pretend, a kind of game, but for Roberto it was bitterly real, a way of life.

"Still missing your girl?" he asked.

Roberto was hard at work. He didn't look up. "I will write Elena tonight," he said. "That will make her seem closer."

"You don't have to stick here with me. You can just pack up and head home."

"That would provide no answers. I would find little work at home at this time of year, and if I'm to get some training so that Elena and I will have a decent life when we marry, I must have money."

It was hard to be this close to need and not be able to help. "Look, Roberto, I could give you a loan."

"You are paying me. That money is being put aside. It will give Elena and me a start."

"But Roberto, I know how homesick you are, how much you're missing Elena and your family...."

"I would rather earn the money. Besides, Doug, you need my help. In this kind of world, you're a babe in the woods."

Douglas hated this image of himself. He was used to feeling competent, in charge, the person who was able to give directions to others. He managed to smile. "You're right. I need a guide." His chagrin showed in his voice.

"Don't feel bad. You can't help it because you weren't born poor. It's a disadvantage most wouldn't mind."

Douglas tried to grin, knowing his friend was only trying to be funny. He had to give Roberto credit. Anybody who'd come up the hard way, struggling every inch as Roberto had, was going to make some jokes about being rich. It was something that made a lot of people feel bitter.

A voice from the past rang in his ears. An old man, who'd been one of the leaders at the church where he'd worked, had told him, "You'll never be really good at this business, young Boyd—not until you've learned to walk in the shoes of those less fortunate. How can you be expected to understand, to touch their need, when you've always had it so easy."

Even six months later, the empathy in that voice made him wince. Well, he'd set out to learn what he'd been told he lacked. With Roberto's help, he was trying to walk in other people's shoes.

But it wasn't easy. There were times when he wanted to take off and run and never be hungry or tired or looked down on again. And the way women like Cathleen reacted to him, successful accomplished women, as though he wasn't quite there . . . as though something was wrong with him. . . . He threw himself into his work, trying to dismiss the thought. What could it matter to him what Cathleen Carroll thought about anything? What could any woman matter to him who couldn't see beneath the surface of things? Still, he couldn't help wondering why she hadn't come back. He glanced toward the house, where only the brown shingled roof was visible, hoping to see her coming from that direction. What was keeping her?

Cath began to feel she'd never be able to get back to the field. It was almost as though Gran were deliberately detaining her.

"Did you check the mail?" Gran asked.

"I'll do that later when I get back from the field." Cath tied the bonnet strings under her chin.

"I wouldn't want to bother you," Gran said, her voice quivering slightly, "but I am anxious to know if we have a letter from your parents."

Cath suppressed a sigh. She had done half a dozen errands since coming to the house to see about Gran, but it was her own strict orders that kept her grandmother from running out to the mailbox to check for herself. If she didn't go, Gran was likely to sneak down there the minute she'd gone back to the field. And until Gran was further down the road to recovery, the sun was too hot for even that short walk. "I'll be right back."

She jogged down the graveled driveway toward the mailbox that stood at the edge of the road. It was easy to understand why her grandmother was anxious to get her mail. Always an active woman until her illness, she found it hard to have to rest and keep quiet. A little mail became an important part of the day.

There was more than a little. Cath discovered a whole stack of letters, catalogs and magazines inside the cavernous rural mailbox. She quickly glanced through them: a letter from her parents and what looked like cards from friends, as well as the usual junk mail. This should cheer Gran up.

She glanced in the direction of the choppers, but she couldn't see anything from this distance. They probably thought she was up here goofing off.

She'd turned to head back toward the house when she heard a noisy roar approaching from the west. A large red automobile was coming toward her.

Not much traffic went past this place. The road came to a dead end down at the McMichaels', so most cars stopped either here or at Whit's. She walked on toward the house, curious about the visitors. She'd just reached the back step when the car swung into the driveway, coughing as though the dust it had stirred up had got into its lungs.

It drew up beside Gran's little car, seemed to gasp and wheeze and then sputtered into silence. Cath tried not to stare at it. It had once been a luxury vehicle, but now it was very old indeed, and in a bad state. One fender was crumpled, there were dents in the hood, and the paint was a scraped and spotted version of what must have once been a glossy red. She was almost sure that had not been the vehicle's original color. The once stately automobile looked like an aging woman who had tried to restore her youth with an unsightly and unsuitable hair color.

Fascinated, Cath stood waiting. These looked like some more of Gran's transients. She'd better head them off before her grandmother got upset again.

To her surprise, a young woman got out of the car. A little girl of five or six clung to her hand, and a wide-eyed baby was balanced on her hip. All three looked tired and hot, their faces rosy from the summer heat.

"Hello," Cath said brightly, trying to sound friendly and welcoming.

No one as much as smiled at her. They just stared with the same look in their wide, dark eyes. The young woman pushed untidy brown hair back from her forehead. "They sent us here," she said.

Cath blinked. "Who sent you?"

The young woman tried to smile, but the motion was hardly more than a trembling of the lips. "Some folks that live up on the highway. They said you were hiring cotton choppers."

Reluctant pity stirred within Cath. Certainly the children were too young to work, the baby appeared barely old enough to walk and the young mother seemed slender and pale, except for the heated flush of her cheeks. She looked as though she was barely managing to stand. How could she work in the fields?

"Mr. McMichaels, the man who's been farming this property, had been looking for workers," she agreed, "but—"

"I'm a real good worker and I need a job bad."

Cath couldn't help feeling Whit would be doing this young woman a favor if he refused to hire her. "It isn't up to me. You'll have to see Mr. McMichaels."

"Can we talk to him, then?"

Cath hesitated, torn between conflicting emotions, but she couldn't resist the appeal in the other woman's eyes. "Just let me show you and the children inside. You can wait while I go get Whit—that's Mr. McMichaels. He's only out in the field."

"I'm thirsty," the little girl said.

"Hush, Mary Ann." With fierce embarrassment, the mother nudged her. "We've got water in the car. You don't have to worry about that."

"But we have fresh milk in the refrigerator." Again Cath smiled at the little girl, who was attractive in spite of the wispy brown hair that looked as if it needed to be combed. She'd feel better if these delicate-looking children had a couple of glasses of wholesome milk inside them.

"Oh, please, Mommy?" Even as if aware the answer would be no, the child looked hopefully up at her parent.

The mother stood stiffly, and Cath was almost certain she would refuse. Then her face relaxed slightly. "If you've plenty, then the children might enjoy a glass each." Her gaze dared the little girl to ask for more. "But I'm not thirsty myself."

In deference to her grandmother's feelings, Cathleen led them to the redwood table that stood in the cool shadow of the rose arbor back of the house. The little girl sighed gratefully at its coolness. "This is nice."

"I've always liked it." Cath couldn't help smiling again. "I'll be right back with the drinks."

She hurried inside. "Did we get a letter?" Gran called.

Cath handed it and the other mail to her. "We've got some visitors out back," she said. "They want to talk to Whit about work, but I'm getting them something cool to drink in the meantime." Her voice sounded breathless and uncertain.

Gran looked at her with sudden sharpness. "More of these vagrants, I suppose. Well, I don't like to think about anybody being hungry if that's what you're hinting at . . . but give them something to eat and send them on their way."

"It's a woman with two small children." Cath was already pouring milk into two glasses and heaping cold cuts and cheese onto thick slices of homemade bread that a neighbor had sent over. She got fruit from a bowl and put it and the other food on a tray. "She doesn't look to be much older than me."

"Probably no better off than she should be." But Gran's voice had softened at the mention of children. She reached for the tray. "I'll take this to them while you go look for Whit."

"But, Gran—"

"Well, where are they?" She peered out the window. "Don't see anything out there but that monster car."

"They're under the arbor. I thought it'd be cooler there."

"Then get going. I'll take care of this."

Cath couldn't feel comfortable with this turn of events. "Don't get too warm," she cautioned. "It isn't good for you."

"I can take care of myself. Scat!"

Cath took off running, but she couldn't help feeling a little anxious about leaving her grandmother alone with strangers. In spite of all her most charitable feelings, she remembered what she'd heard about robberies and burglaries and other crimes being committed by the desperate workers stranded in the area by the aftermath of the oil boom. And Gran was certainly in no condition to stand up for herself, even against the young woman she'd left in the shade of the rose arbor.

Whit's pickup was nowhere in sight as Cath dashed up to where Roberto and Douglas were so hard at work that at first they weren't even aware of her presence. "Where's Whit?" she yelled even before she reached them.

She couldn't help being aware of Douglas's expression as he looked up and saw her, warmth flooding the unusual light-blue eyes. Then, almost as if that warmth had been a breach of courtesy, a formal surface concealed it. "He said something about going to check on his calves."

"He's not at the barn, so he must have headed back to his own place." Anxiously she glanced toward the house. She didn't want to leave Gran alone any longer. "Look, would one of you mind driving over and telling Whit I need to see him?"

"I'll do it." Douglas dropped his hoe and headed for the van.

His friend regarded her with a worried look. "What is it? Is something wrong with your grandmother?"

Abruptly, Cath realized the impression she must have given, springing out here this way and demanding to see Whit immediately. "Oh no, it's nothing like that. There's someone else looking for work, a young woman with two children."

Roberto grinned. "I think your grandmother will not be pleased."

Cath shook her head. "She's one tough lady. She's out back feeding them milk and sandwiches right now."

He grinned appreciation. "Still, Cath, it is sad, but these days one must be cautious about trusting strangers. I'll go back with you until Whit arrives."

They went toward the house together, and it wasn't until they were almost there that Cathleen realized that Roberto and Douglas already seemed like her friends, even though yesterday they were strangers.

Chapter Four

Even as Cath jogged into the yard, she could hear voices raised in anger. Her heart stepped up its beat. "I shouldn't have left Gran here alone with strangers!"

"Your grandmother is okay," Roberto assured her, pointing to where Gran stood with the dark-haired young woman, just outside the rose arbor.

Quickly, Cath ran toward them, but her grandmother didn't seem in need of her protection.

"I'll have you know, it's quite out of the question," she was telling the young woman in no-nonsense tones, sounding more like herself than she had in months.

Cath glanced inside the arbor where the little girl was tilting a glass of milk toward her younger sister's eager mouth, more of it spilling down the baby's bare chest than going inside. Both children were seated on the grass, and the smaller one had a cookie clutched in her hand.

She turned her attention back to the adults. "Now, Mrs. Price," Roberto said, gently taking control of the situation. "Your granddaughter is concerned that you are overexerting yourself. Let's sit down and talk like reasonable people."

"I'm fine," Gran assured them, but she allowed Roberto to lead her to the picnic table within the arbor, where she sank down on a bench, fanning herself with one hand. "Sure is hot," she said, then glared again at the young woman with whom she'd been arguing. "Too hot to think of staying in a chicken house."

The woman had moved into the arbor with them, but she didn't sit down. She stood in front of Mrs. Price, her face set in a determined expression. "It's only because chickens used to live in it that you feel that way. Actually, it looks to be a well-built little house. People all over the world live in worse."

Cath frowned. What was this about? Why were they arguing over the chicken house? She didn't get a chance to ask because just then two vehicles, the old van and Whit's pickup, both roared into the yard. She grinned. The troops were coming. Doubtless they were going to be disappointed to learn that the only crisis was a frail-looking young woman and two small children!

Douglas came dashing up, several feet in advance of the heavier Whit. "What's wrong? Is Mrs. Price all right?"

Cath's grandmother regarded him with open disapproval. "I'm fine," she said. "I don't know what everybody's making such a fuss about."

Whit came puffing up, looking like an out-of-condition football player. "Mrs. Price! Cath! What's going on here?"

Cath shrugged. "Sorry, Whit, didn't mean to make you think it was an emergency."

"Is this Mr. McMichaels?" the young woman asked quietly.

Cath nodded.

"I'm the emergency, Mr. McMichaels. I'm looking for work and was told you might need someone to help with chopping cotton."

Whit's kindly face stared doubtfully at her. Then he looked at Cath. "I don't hardly think . . ."

"I'm accustomed to hard work, Mr. McMichaels, and I need a job badly."

"Doesn't take no for an answer," Mrs. Price informed them grumpily. "Wants to live in my chicken house, if you can believe that."

Cath shook her head in amazement. "Why would anyone want to live in your chicken house, Gran?"

"Well, don't act as though I'm making it up! Ask her. That's what she said, that she wanted to live in my chicken house."

The young woman turned to Cath, sticking out her hand. "I'm Sylvia Marlowe," she said, speaking as though they'd been introduced at a formal gathering. "These are my daughters, Mary Ann and Kristina."

"I'm Mary Ann," the older child told them gravely. "I'm six, but Kristina is only one. She's just a baby."

Sylvia Marlowe smoothed the skirt of a dress too hot for a warm summer's day. It looked as though it might be made of wool. Cath wondered if she'd worn it because it was her only presentable dress. "The reason I asked about the chicken house is that I'm looking for a suitable place to rent for a short while."

"A chicken house isn't suitable," Cath's grandmother told her. "And I won't hear another word about it."

Cath couldn't help being alarmed about the rosy glow along Gran's cheekbones. This was too much for a recovering invalid. "Why don't you go inside, Gran. We can manage without you."

Her grandmother regarded her with an icy stare. "If I do that, first thing I know people will be living in my chicken house."

"Well, Mrs. Price, it isn't like you're planning to keep chickens in there," Whit said in an attempt at humor that made no one smile.

Douglas stepped only slightly forward, but Cath was sure that everyone there was as suddenly aware of his presence as she was. "Mrs. Marlowe, I think what Mrs. Price is having trouble understanding is why anyone would want to rent a building that she sees as fit only for animals. You might try explaining to her."

Cath was abruptly reminded of the old van and her suspicion that the two men lived inside it. "There's not much rental property in this area," she said quickly.

Sylvia Marlowe nodded, her flushed face highlighted by dark eyes and hair. "And what there is I can't afford right now. And if I'm to work for Mr. McMichaels, then I'll need some place nearby for the girls and me to stay." Her eyes focused again on the elderly woman. "It would only be for a few days."

"Haven't heard Whit say he'd hire you. How are you going to work in the field with those babies?"

"I'm not a baby," Mary Ann announced with indignation. "I already told you I was six. I'm going to be in first grade."

"And you used to tell me how you took your children to the field with you when you and Grandad were getting started," Cath reminded her grandmother. "You said they'd take naps or play in the shade while you worked."

"It was necessary then. Those were hard times."

"For some people, Mrs. Price, these are hard times," Douglas said quietly.

"I'm talking about the Depression. Everybody was having it tough." She disregarded him, looking again at Sylvia. "You don't look well. You should leave the working to your man."

"Daddy went away," Mary Ann informed her gravely. "I don't think he loves us anymore."

"Mary Ann!" her mother spoke sharply, then faced the older woman again, as though aware the answer to both her problems—housing and employment—rested with her. "I am responsible for myself and my daughters. I'll take care of us."

Cath touched her grandmother's arm. "Gran, I could sleep on the sofa for a few days. They could have my room."

Her grandmother didn't even look at her. "I'll not have strangers in my house."

Cath started to protest, but Douglas caught her attention, frowning slightly at her as though to warn her to silence.

The two principal contestants faced each other. Finally, Mrs. Price's gaze dropped. "It really isn't a bad chicken house," she finally admitted, sounding thoughtful. "It's built good, nice and tight so the rain won't come in, and it's clean. I scrubbed it out regularly myself until I got sick. Even got a place for a light bulb in the ceiling so you'd have a light at least."

"But, Gran," Cath protested, unable to believe she was seriously considering it. "There's no water, no place to cook, no bathroom!"

"I can remember when none of the houses around here had indoor plumbing," her grandmother informed her. "And she's welcome to draw water from the old cistern."

"We have a camp stove in the trunk of the car," Sylvia Marlowe added quickly, as though afraid the offer would be withdrawn. "We've been camping out at the park in town, but the authorities have decided to forbid the tents."

Cath decided not to say anything more. Obviously the well-constructed little building, which hadn't housed chickens in more than a decade, offered substantially more protection than a tent. Besides, help would be close at hand in case Sylvia and her two children needed it.

"Whit can take the rent out of what he pays you for chopping cotton," Gran told Sylvia, "and if you'll come with me, I've got an old mattress and some old blankets that you can use."

Sylvia didn't move. "We don't need charity."

"It's part of the rent, so I can charge you more."

Cath found herself grinning up at Doug as she watched a hesitant Sylvia being herded toward the house by her grandmother. "Never a dull moment," she said.

His smile flooded her with warmth. "I can tell that."

Whit shook his head. "Guess I've got me another cotton chopper, though I'm not sure how she'll hold up."

"Mommy's been sick," Mary Ann told him gravely. "That's why she lost her job."

Cath would have liked to question the child, to find out more about the family's situation, but it hardly seemed fair. "I'm sure she'll get better now," she told the little girl, hoping it was true. She couldn't help thinking how hot the sun had felt out in that cotton field.

"Hope so," Whit said, shaking his head again. "You and your grandmother, Cath, are always getting me into something."

"Perhaps we should get back to work," suggested Roberto, who had been silent for some time.

Whit nodded. "That's a right good idea." He hesitated, however, looking first at Cath, then at the house where her grandmother had vanished with Sylvia Marlowe. "I don't know about leaving you alone, though…" He stopped, looking down at the little girl with obvious embarrassment.

It was easy to read his mind. He was still suspicious of the woman, afraid she might be some kind of con artist who would do them harm if he left them alone. "Tell you what," he finally said, "we'll get back to the field after it gets cooler. Right now why don't we go down and take a look at that chicken house and see if it needs a few repairs here and there. We wouldn't want these little girls to get wet if it started to rain."

Roberto followed him across the yard toward the cluster of buildings in the barnyard, but Douglas stayed at Cath's side, staring after them with some bewilderment. "It's hard to believe there are people who are happy to get a chance to live in a chicken house," he said in a low voice.

Cath stared at his face, resisting an impulse to reach out and touch his arm, which was so close to her own. What kind of man was he that he lived in an old van and yet was surprised at other people's poverty?

She told herself she was spending too much time considering the puzzle that was Douglas Boyd. Bending over, she picked up the baby, balancing her on one hip as her mother had done, and reached out a hand to the older child. "Come on, Mary Ann and Kristina, let's go inside and wash some of the cookie and milk off your faces. Then maybe a nap will feel good."

"I never take naps," Mary Ann assured her. "I'm a big girl."

Douglas turned to watch them go toward the house, the lovely young woman whose hair shone in the blazing morning sun and the two children. Then he turned to look back at the chicken house.

He couldn't help thinking about the house where he'd grown up. It had been an old Georgian mansion, comfortable and pretentious at the same time, a house that said something about its residents—and about old money that didn't have to build a new and fancy residence to make a statement. The Boyd family had reached that place in society where they didn't have to make statements. Other people wanted to impress them.

He shook his head. Not that he'd ever analyzed it, not back then. The big old house had simply been his home, and he'd loved it. Most of his friends had equally luxurious homes. He supposed, if he ever thought about it, that this was the way of life.

A chicken house! Maybe that elder who'd tried to analyze his situation had been right. He did have a few things to learn.

"Douglas!" Roberto's shout brought him out of his contemplation. "Come on, we need your help."

He hurried toward them.

Cath found herself thinking of Douglas Boyd as she washed dirty faces and sticky hands. Then she took her brush and gently began to untangle Mary Ann's brown hair while the baby explored the bedroom under her watchful eye.

"We have to be careful of Kristina," Mary Ann told her. "She doesn't know not to put things in her mouth."

Cath found that instead of her mind staying firmly on those two unfortunate children, it had a tendency to roam to the subject of one tall, broad-shouldered young man. She couldn't help thinking how it would feel to be very close to him, so close that she could reach out and touch his face with her hand and then he would...

Abruptly she forced herself to focus on what was going on around her. It was a little embarrassing to discover herself daydreaming about a member of the opposite sex like a boy-crazy fifteen-year-old. She forced her mind back onto a more acceptable track. "Do you help look after your sister, Mary Ann?"

"Sometimes. Mommy always got a baby-sitter when she had to work, but they didn't always take good care of Kristina. So I had to watch her."

No wonder the child seemed so oddly grave for a six-year-old. Poor baby, she'd had to be grown up, as did so many children. Cath couldn't help thinking about equally sad stories she'd heard at the hospital where she worked. Children who were hurt through neglect or even deliberately injured were, unfortunately, not a novelty these days.

"Kristina is lucky to have a big sister like you," she told the little girl. Even though Gran might disapprove, she tucked the two little girls into her own bed, giving them only a light sheet for covering, and adjusting the fan so that a breeze would refresh the room. "Just take a rest," she said, "then you'll feel better."

"I don't take naps," Mary Ann reminded her firmly. "I'm a big girl."

"But you can stay with your sister until she falls asleep," Cath said, sitting down in a nearby chair and picking up a book. Mary Ann went to sleep even before her sister and Cath got up and crept out of the room, anxious to find out what was going on.

"Where is everybody?" she called from the back step.

"Down here." Douglas stuck his head out the door of the chicken house.

She walked across the yard, prepared to scold her grandmother for being out in the heat again, but was surprised to find Douglas alone in the chicken house. Proudly, he displayed its changed interior to her. The mattress Gran had mentioned was raised from the floor by an old iron bedstead so that it stood in one corner looking like a regular bed, complete with pillows and blankets. An old wooden rocker stood at the other end. Cath thought it had been discarded years ago. Next to it was a small table that had been in the living room a few minutes ago. A small supply of magazines, a couple of books and a prominently displayed arrangements of silk flowers sat on top of it.

Douglas grinned. "Your grandmother may not approve, but she's gone out of her way to make this chicken house look homey."

She frowned at him. He certainly had no business being amused by Gran, who had only tried to be kind in spite of her own fears. "You've got to understand how it is. She's been sick and her whole world seems to be changing. The home of one of her friends was burglarized only last week. She's afraid, and she has a right to be."

"I didn't mean to say anything to the contrary."

She glared at him, more angry at herself for the way she couldn't seem to keep him off her mind than for anything he'd said. She knew she was being unreasonable, and that made her so mad that she couldn't keep quiet. "It may be hard for you to identify with an older person, someone who's so different from you, but you should try." She found herself staring at him, disconcerted by her own vehemence over practically nothing. She would have smiled if anyone else had described such a reaction to a virtual stranger. Chemistry, she would have said simply. Pure and simple attraction. She wanted to deny what she was feeling.

His smile was gentle and a little too knowing, as though he could see into her mind and read her turbulent thoughts. "Not everyone fits into this neat domestic world you and your grandmother envision."

It was a strange remark. "Oh, I'm sure you're a jungle creature, much too adventurous to be happy in our farmyard."

"Undoubtedly." He nodded solemnly. "I'm out here living a riotous life, chopping cotton, fixing up chicken houses and generally having a great time. My life is full of excitement.''

He had a right to complain. He'd practically begged for the job yesterday. She found herself speechless.

"Don't misunderstand. I don't mind having a good influence around here."

He was making fun of her. Cath straightened, trying to regain some sense of dignity. It wasn't easy. For some reason she felt ridiculous, as though her own pretensions were foolish. He made her feel as though she were trying to set herself up as some sort of standard, a kind of Lady Bountiful, who was stooping to those less fortunate than herself to do good. That wasn't the way it was. She didn't want to be like that.

For about the hundredth time that summer, she wished she were in Mexico. Everything here seemed too complicated. If she'd gone down there to work with the medical team, helping to teach prenatal and neonatal care, she wouldn't be feeling so mixed up, doubting herself and this weird obsession she seemed to have for a man she wasn't even sure she liked.

Right now she was uncomfortably aware of a compulsion to reach out and smooth his hair, which had been ruffled by the breeze. It had a springy texture, the kind of hair that didn't stay long in place, and she already knew how it would feel under her fingers.

Suddenly appalled at her own thoughts, she decided it was time to put him in his place. "After you've finished here, you might draw a bucket of water up from the cistern for Mrs. Marlowe and the girls to use," she said pleasantly, trying to sound business-like, employer to employee.

He got the message. "Be happy to do that, Miss Carroll."

She felt sure he still wasn't taking her all that seriously. She saw his hand move upward, then drop again and had a feeling he'd come close to giving her a mock salute. In exasperation, she started out of the chicken house, determined that from now on she would keep the lines between them firmly drawn. She'd taken only a few steps toward the house when she remembered the reason she'd come down in the first place. The man seemed to drive all rational thought from her brain!

She turned to find him standing in the doorway, watching her depart. Color flooded her face at the intensity in those unusual eyes of his. "Where is everybody?" she asked, too shaken even to attempt dignity. "What's happened to my grandmother?"

"She went with the others."

"But where did they go?"

"Over to Whit's place. He had some things over there they could use to fix up this place."

"What kinds of things?" she asked, puzzled.

"Camping equipment, a chemical toilet and some dishes and pans."

Cath couldn't help frowning. "I don't see why Gran had to go. She has no business running around in this heat."

He grinned at her. "That's what Whit said, but she doesn't mind too well."

She couldn't help smiling back. "No, she certainly doesn't."

They were both startled when a piercing scream sounded from the direction of the house. "The children!" Cath yelled, already in motion.

But he was faster and dashed past her. He was already going in through the back door when another scream sounded.

Cath's heart pounded. Even as she ran, horrible visions flashed through her head. Had the baby fallen, or gotten into something dangerous? What could be wrong?

"Mary Ann?" she called as she entered the house. She raced through to the bedroom, where she found Douglas bending over two sobbing children.

"It's all right," he soothed. "Everything's all right."

Cath clutched at his arm. "What is it? What's happened to them?"

He pulled the baby onto his lap and patted the head of the wide-eyed Mary Ann. Cath was able to breathe easier now that she could see that both children were unharmed.

Her knees were jelly. She sank down onto the bed beside them.

"I guess I had a nightmare," Mary Ann confessed in a tiny, embarrassed voice. "It happens sometimes."

Douglas comforted her in a calming voice. "Everybody has bad dreams now and then." Little Kristina still sobbed and he cuddled her closer. "I used to have some lollapaloozas when I was a kid."

"What's a lollapa...what's that?" Mary Ann asked, distracted.

"It's a real wingding fantastical dream, the kind that makes you sit straight up in the middle of your bed," he assured her solemnly.

"The kind where you dream monsters are about to get you?"

"Is that what you dreamed, Mary Ann?" Cath asked. Her hands were still shaking so that she had to clench them into fists. She envied Douglas for his poise.

The little girl nodded. "Great big, ugly monsters. They were going to get me, and I kept calling to my daddy. I wanted my daddy, but he wouldn't come."

The smaller child seemed calm now, and Cath took her from Douglas, finding some comfort herself in holding the little body against her chest. "I'm sure your dad will be home soon, Mary Ann. He must miss you."

Large brown eyes looked straight into her own. "I don't think he's ever coming back."

Douglas reached over to tug playfully at one rather limp curl. "If I had a nice family like this, I'd be in a big hurry to get back to them, I can promise you that, Mary Ann."

That earnest gaze switched from Cathleen to him. "Daddy said he'd be back for my birthday. That's today. If he doesn't come by the time I go to sleep tonight, then I'll know he's never coming."

Involuntarily, Cath closed her eyes. Her birthday. Poor baby.

"You mean you're six today?" Douglas asked, as though that was a momentous fact.

The little girl nodded. "And if my daddy doesn't come back for my birthday, it must be because I've been really bad."

"Oh, no, honey," Cath said. "There has to be some other reason."

"He'd be here if he could," Douglas said, adding his assurance. "I'm certain there must be something very important to keep him away."

"You mean like he's dead?"

Douglas looked to Cathleen in appeal. "Mary Ann's daddy would expect us to do something in his place to celebrate her birthday," she suggested.

"Of course." He grasped quickly at the idea. "What could we do?"

"Well, I can tell you how we celebrated my birthday when I was about her age." Cath pretended to address herself to Douglas, but both of them had their eyes on the child, hoping she was being distracted from her fears about her father. "Gran always let us have a hot dog roast."

"A hot dog roast? What's that?" Mary Ann asked. Kristina bounced enthusiastically on Cath's lap, burbling unintelligible sounds.

"We'd go down on the other side of the pond where that grove of trees is, and we'd build a fire by the edge of the water, where it wouldn't catch the grass or woods on fire. And then we'd cut off a few green sticks from the trees and sharpen the ends. We'd stick hot dogs on them and hold them over the fire until they were nice and hot and delicious."

"Can I hold a hot dog over the fire my own self?"

Cath looked at Douglas and smiled with relief.

"I believe it could be arranged, Mary Ann," he said.

Suddenly they heard a voice call from the front part of the house. "Cath, Sylvia is ready to get the children settled into their new home now."

"We're back here in my room, Gran," Cath called.

A moment later, Mrs. Price and Sylvia appeared in the doorway. Mary Ann ran to her mother. "We're going to have a hot dog roast, Mommy, and I get to hold the stick over the fire."

Sylvia Marlowe's pale face held a little more color now, but she still looked strained. "A fire?" she echoed. "What are you talking about, Mary Ann?"

The baby babbled some meaningless sounds, holding her arms out to her mother, and Cath handed her over.

"We just learned that today is Mary Ann's birthday, Gran," she explained hastily, "so I thought we might have a hot dog roast down by the pond the way we used to."

Her grandmother didn't say anything, but just stood looking past Cath to where Douglas was still seated on the bed. Quickly, he rose to his feet. "Guess I'd better go see what Whit wants me to do next," he said.

Gran didn't move out of the doorway. "You just tell Whit that, no matter what, by six o'clock I'm going to need you to help with this outing Cath has planned. Don't want my pasture burning down or something."

He grinned. "I'll be glad to help, Mrs. Price."

But when he and Sylvia Marlowe's little family had all left, Gran turned to Cath with a serious expression. "We should do what we can to help the unfortunates of this world, Cathleen, but that doesn't mean we have to fall in love with them."

Cath felt her face grow warm. "I'm not falling in love with anybody, Gran."

"Just see to it that it stays that way." Gran's eyes were full of concern.

Chapter Five

That evening Cathleen walked down with Douglas to the pond to prepare for the evening's festivities. She couldn't help feeling a little self-conscious after her grandmother's warning. If her feelings were that transparent, then even he might be able to see them.

"It was nice of you to suggest a party for the little girl," he said, sounding as though he felt as awkward as she did at this moment. "You did really well managing that whole thing, in fact. I've never been around children much and didn't have any idea what to do or say."

"I've worked with sick children," she said, disclaiming credit, "but I was as much at a loss about what to do as you. Poor little kid. She seems to think it's her fault that her dad left."

"I've heard that kids blame themselves when things go wrong. I was talking to her mom while we were getting the chicken house fixed up...."

"We've got to quit calling it that," she said, grinning.

He nodded. "The present residence of the Marlowe family," he corrected, sounding very New England and formal.

She wondered exactly where he came from and what had brought him here. He didn't seem like the kind of man who wandered around looking for odd jobs, but then neither did his friend, Roberto. Maybe there was no such type. "What did Sylvia have to say?"

"Not much. I told her about Mary Ann's nightmare and how she was screaming in her sleep. She just looked sad and said it had been happening a lot lately. I suggested that maybe it would help if the family got together again."

"Oh, Douglas, you didn't! That's invading her privacy."

His face took on a stubborn set. "Don't care, not if it helps. Sometimes people get so caught up in their own lives that they can't see what's happening to the people they love. A little counsel will sometimes shake them loose."

Cathleen couldn't help feeling exasperated. "But who do you think you are to be counseling them?"

"Who am I, indeed!" he said with astonishment, then shut his mouth abruptly.

"I'm sorry. I didn't mean to insult you. It's just that, working as a nurse, I've seen the results of people who haven't the training trying to interfere in other people's lives."

Douglas seemed amused. "Honestly, I wasn't trying to interfere, Cathleen. Sylvia just looks as though she's carrying a weight of trouble that's too big for her, and I wanted to help."

Cath was shocked at the twinge of jealousy she felt. But then, the young Mrs. Marlowe was quite attractive with her big eyes and pathetic appearance, just the type some gallant male might want to rescue. She frowned at her own thoughts. How nasty-tempered she was being these days. Sylvia Marlowe had a husband somewhere. And besides, why should it matter to her who Douglas was interested in?

"We always had our fires out on that tip of land which sticks out into the pond," she said, pointing. "That way the flames are easy to confine."

He nodded and bent over to pick up a fallen log. "Lots of deadwood down here. We won't have any trouble getting enough."

"We haven't had an outing down here in years. The last one I remember was when I was in high school, and we had such a good time. Gran invited a bunch of area kids, Whit included, of course. After we ate, one of the guys played a guitar and we sat around and sang old songs." She laughed. "Real sophisticated fun."

She looked from the pastures, where twilight would soon be adding its soft haze to the landscape, to the small white frame house on the hill across the road. This place was a second home to her, more dear in some ways than the urban neighborhood where she'd grown up, or the attractive little apartment she'd furnished with her salary from the hospital.

If her plans materialized, her opportunities to come back here might be limited. She'd been on the brink of a big career step when the position she'd worked for and dreamed about for so long had been offered, but she'd had to turn it down to come here. Some other nurse had gotten the opportunity to take the place meant for her on the speciality medical team that would be working at the forefront in offering care for those high-risk newborns who'd once had so little chance at life. The trip to Mexico had been only the beginning of what would have been a unique opportunity, but she'd had little choice but to come here instead.

Now that Gran was getting better, she felt a sudden impatience to get on with her life, to get out of this trap that kept her connected with the past, and move on into the future.

"Guess we'd better gather some wood," Douglas said, interrupting her thoughts with his practical comment.

She began adding sticks to the small pile of wood he'd already started. "We'll need a big fire. I want Mary Ann to be impressed."

"The thing that would please her most right now is finding her father."

Cath shrugged. "Not much we can do about that if he's chosen to abandon his family."

"I wonder, though, if that's the real story."

She stared incredulously at him. "What else can it be?"

"I don't know but I'm going to find out."

Cath couldn't help wondering if his concern was for the child, or for her mother. Maybe he just wanted to make sure there was no husband to come back into the picture and complicate matters.

Oops! That little edge of jealousy was moving its way back into her mind. She recognized how unreasonable she was being. She didn't want him, yet she didn't want anyone else to have him either. Cath found she didn't like herself much these days.

It was funny because a month ago she'd been fairly pleased with herself. Not every young woman was about to go out and do something as vital as the work she'd chosen, helping to save lives. But it had come as a shock when she realized that the service called for was somewhat less dramatic; just looking after the grandmother she loved for the summer. Nobody was going to pin any medals on her for doing that.

Cath frowned. But surely that wasn't her motivation for choosing to be a nurse. Not for attention, or to be admired, her reasons were better than that. She tried to count them. She was ambitious. She did like recognition; otherwise, she might not have climbed so quickly up the career ladder at the huge hospital. But she'd chosen nursing, originally, because it was meaningful work. She really had wanted to help people.

She sighed. It all sounded a little vague and fuzzy. What had happened to the sense of purpose that she'd started with? She could still remember the night back when she was nineteen and she'd heard a local doctor speak at a college class. He'd spoken of the exciting new developments in neonatal care, of the babies who once would have been condemned to certain death, or at best brief and tragic lives, but who would now have, at least, a chance, thanks to modern medicine. She'd wanted to be a part of that.

"Cathleen." The deep voice penetrated through the haze of her thoughts. For just an instant she couldn't think whose voice it was.

She turned, then smiled. "Douglas, I'm sorry. Guess I really tuned out."

He went over to sit on the grassy bank of the pond, patting the ground at his side. "Come on, sit down and tell me what's bothering you."

She didn't stop to think that he was assuming a lot. Something in his manner told her he was used to listening. But she was oddly shy. "We don't have time. We have to get ready for the party."

"You can afford to take a couple of minutes off."

Without further protest, she joined him on the grass. She didn't say anything at first, but sat quietly, watching a nearby grasshopper. It seemed to reflect for a moment, then took a giant hop that carried it off into taller grass. She looked up at him. His clear blue eyes were studying her, a look of amusement and affection in them.

It was as though she'd always known him. She felt that she could tell him things she'd never dare say to another person and that he would understand. "Where do you come from?" she asked. "Where is your home?"

It was as though a cloud passed over his eyes. "I've traveled a lot, though I've lived in San Antonio for most of the last few years."

"But you're not a native Texan?"

He shook his head. "I grew up in Connecticut."

"You're a long way from home."

He smiled. "We're supposed to be talking about you, not me."

She grinned, preparing to challenge that statement. "But you're so much more interesting."

"Not me. I've lived a very dull life."

"Somehow I doubt that, and I'm an expert; my life is the dull one."

"Can't see why you say that."

"You've seen what it's like out here—very ordinary. It's the same at home. I have two brothers, both of them older, nice parents, a good job. Tell me how you find drama in any of that."

His laughter rang softly across the pond, not even disturbing a cluster of ducks swimming on the far side. "You sound so glum about your good fortune. What do you want out of life, major tragedy and suffering?"

Obviously he was not sympathetic to her problem. She regarded him with open disapproval. "I'd like to think there's some point to things, that I was accomplishing something."

He was looking at her as though she were as young as Mary Ann. Abruptly he reached out, touching the corner of her lips with one finger. "You're so sweet and funny," he said.

The gesture seemed too natural for her to be startled. "You're not taking me seriously," she protested.

The amusement vanished from his eyes. "I've never taken anyone more seriously in my life, and the timing's never been so rotten."

"What do you mean?"

He didn't answer, and the silence around them was broken only by the cry of birds in the grove that ringed the pond. From somewhere in the distance, Cath heard a voice, someone calling, but it seemed a million miles away. Already the sizzling heat was beginning to cool into her favorite time of day. Evening was magic out here, shadowed with night and silvered with moon and stars that always seemed brighter than they possibly could be when in competition with the artificial glow of a large city.

Their gazes met and some natural energy crackled between them. Cath closed her eyes and leaned away, suddenly frightened by the unexpected fire she saw in his eyes. What was happening to them?

"Doug! Cath! Where are you?"

Douglas looked up with irritation as the voice he'd heard only vaguely before sounded from closer range. He didn't want to be interrupted, not now. He turned his eyes again to her, studying the face of the young woman sitting on the grass across from him, seeing the sensitive features, the large, alarmed-looking eyes. Instinctively he reached toward her, feeling almost compelled to draw her close to him, to hold her safe within his arms.

He heard someone crashing through the trees behind them. "Douglas?"

It was the voice of his friend Roberto, his companion in this adventure, that brought him back to reality. This was not the time to let himself fall for any woman, and particularly not Cathleen Carroll, who tried to hide her contempt for his status even from herself.

"We're over here, Roberto," he called, getting up and brushing wisps of grass from the legs of his jeans. He extended a helping hand in Cathleen's direction.

She stared at it as though wondering at his intention. "Let me help you get up."

At the invitation, she grasped his hand and he pulled her effortlessly to her feet. The only trouble was that he had the hardest time remembering to release her hand, so they stood there clinging to each other until Roberto came running up to them.

"I've been looking all over for you," he told them, sounding slightly cross. "Cathleen, your grandmother wants you to go to the store before it closes and get some things for the party."

Douglas frowned at his friend. "She won't have time to go all the way into town."

"There's a little store only a couple of miles from here where I can get everything we'll need," she told him. "Guess I'd better hurry. Roberto can help you get the wood."

She was already in motion, and he couldn't help thinking grimly that she was suddenly very anxious to get away from him.

She was almost out of sight in the little woods when she called to them. "Both of you have to come to the party, of course. Mary Ann will expect you."

Until now he'd had no other thought but that they'd be expected to participate in the little girl's party. The invitation was a bitter reminder of their status here.

He stalked away from the pond, back into the trees and started picking up fallen wood. Roberto followed him.

"Doug, are you all right?"

"I'm fine."

"You look mad."

"I'm not mad, I'm fine," Douglas insisted angrily, whacking a small log down onto the pile of wood so hard that the whole pile seemed to jump.

Roberto nodded wisely. "It's getting to you, my reverend friend."

Roberto hadn't called him that in weeks. "Perhaps a little," he admitted.

When they'd first met and Roberto had accidentally discovered that he was a minister, the barrier between them had seemed impossible to bridge. Douglas, lonely and confused in the new world of drifting workers, had confided his problem, not so much because he really wanted help, but because he'd seen it as a way to lend assistance to someone who would never have accepted it as an outright gift. It was a way of being able to provide income that would give Roberto and his fiancée a better start in life. But he'd been wiser than he'd known and Roberto had a better teacher than he'd had a right to expect.

He'd long since stopped regarding the relationship as a simple business arrangement and had considered it an accomplishment when the younger man had started addressing him by his first name, even when they were alone. It meant they were friends and equals. Now he couldn't set back that friendship by being less than honest.

"I didn't count on some of the factors," Douglas said.

"Miss Carroll?"

"You've been calling her Cath. Why so formal all of a sudden?"

"Even when they say, 'Roberto, call me by my first name,' still there is a barrier between us. I am the hired help, and they look at me differently."

Douglas kicked angrily at the log. "That's ridiculous, Roberto. You're an intelligent and gifted young man with a promising future. Nobody should look down on you."

A certain bitterness crept into Roberto's features. "Most of them don't see who I am; they only see what I am, a migrant worker." Suddenly he laughed. "Don't be so concerned, Doug. It doesn't matter to me, not anymore. I have Elena and she loves me. All the other girls in the world can look at me as though

I'm beneath their notice, and it won't matter. Only Elena matters."

Douglas was beginning to understand the feeling. It would be so easy to substitute another name in that statement and to say "only Cathleen matters."

"But not her, not Cathleen," he argued. "She isn't like those others you're talking about. She looks past the surface to the individual underneath. Look how good she's being to Sylvia and her little girls."

Roberto looked as though he didn't want to debate the matter. "She's very nice, Douglas. I wasn't criticizing her. She's just like most people...."

"No she isn't. She's different."

"If you say so."

"No, she's really different. She's kind and good and intelligent."

Roberto looked down at the ground rather than at Douglas. "And quite beautiful. Are you sure that isn't why you want to believe she's all those other things as well?"

"What do you mean?" Douglas stared at him, almost compelling him to look up.

"My Elena is gentle and loving, but no one would call her beautiful. I overlooked her at first; she was someone I took for granted until finally I really saw her. This is how I know it's truly love. But this Cathleen, she is tall and golden, very lovely, not easy to overlook."

"That's nonsense!" Douglas felt a pounding at his temples.

"No it is not. You are feeling a stirring of the senses and you want to believe the storybooks that say the princess will look past the surface, past the menial, and see someone wonderful there. If you want to win this girl, then go into town and buy fine clothes and a good car. Tell her who you are and how rich your family is, and then she will see that you are the kind of man she is allowed to admire."

"But Cathleen's not like that." He switched back to the original point of the debate.

"You want to believe that, my friend."

Douglas stared at his friend aghast. Roberto had always seemed lighthearted, optimistic in spite of his circumstances. Douglas had had no idea of the depths of bitterness hidden beneath the surface. "Do you think I'm like that, too, Roberto?" he asked quietly.

"At first I thought so." Suddenly the young man grinned, showing an engaging flash of teeth. "But then I see that you are truly trying to overcome the obstacle of being wealthy."

Douglas couldn't help laughing. "It isn't my money. It belongs to my family."

"And they'll let you have some as long as you behave yourself."

"That's about it." Douglas didn't bother to point out that he hadn't called on the resources of his family since finishing college, that he'd lived entirely on the modest salary his church had paid him to serve as youth minister. But to Roberto, who had known real hardship, that salary might not seem so modest. And even now, when he was choosing to live this life of hardship, always in the back of his mind was the knowledge that all he had to do was call home to get help.

But that would be an admission of failure, showing his family that they'd been right all along and that this religion thing was just a stage he was going through. His mouth set into a firm line at the thought. He would be thirty in a few more months; even Dad would have to consider that an adult age and admit that his professional choice was something more than a youthful phase. No, no matter how bad things got, he wouldn't give up.

They didn't talk about it anymore, but quickly gathered up an adequate supply of wood. Afterward they allowed themselves a few minutes for a quick wash, not in the muddy little pond, but in the clear springwater that fed into it from a little stream. "Hard to stay clean when you live in a van," Douglas said. "Let's go put on some fresh clothes and get ready for Mary Ann's party."

"Don't you know that people like us just don't care about being clean?" Roberto asked cynically.

Douglas only grinned. He was going to ignore his friend's skepticism tonight and concentrate on having a good time. No matter what Roberto thought, he was sure he'd never met a woman like Cathleen Carroll before.

That night she looked even lovelier than he'd remembered when they gathered by the dying embers of what had been a good-sized fire. Mary Ann chattered incessantly as she stuck her hot dog out over the flames, under the watchful eye of Mrs. Price.

In turn, Cath kept a watchful eye on her grandmother. "I still don't think you should have come down here," she said, protesting. "It isn't smart to overdo it when you've just been so sick."

"Don't be foolish," her grandmother said firmly. "It's getting so you think everything I might enjoy is bad for me, Cathleen. If I'm going to die, let me have a good time doing it."

"But I don't want you to die," Cath said, sounding so like a little girl that Douglas wanted to go and comfort her. He resisted the temptation, his gaze going automatically to Roberto, who was dispensing cold sodas from a tub of ice. Roberto thought Cathleen wouldn't be interested in a person of his apparent station in life. Douglas rejected the thought. Cathleen wasn't like that. Just this afternoon, he'd sensed her response to his presence. She was drawn to him, as he was to her. It was something natural and right.

"I don't plan to die anytime soon," Mrs. Price said, giving her granddaughter an affectionate look. "Now quit hovering and have a little fun."

Obediently, Cathleen looked around, her gaze settling first on Douglas, then moving quickly on. She went to the opposite side of the fire, where Sylvia Marlowe sat on a log, her younger daughter held in her lap. "Having a good time, Sylvia?" Douglas heard her ask.

"It's very nice, so good of you to do this for Mary Ann."

Properly grateful was the thought that flashed into his mind. Sylvia Marlowe didn't like to accept help, so it was a little hard to say thanks, but she was doing it because of the obvious excitement and pleasure of her child. He shook his head, staring into the fire. This whole situation was such a puzzle that he didn't know what to think anymore. Even the members of his family, who seemed to have few religious convictions, believed in an obligation to those who unfortunately were unable to care for themselves.

And he had often heard such concern urged from the pulpit, had spoken the words himself. But Roberto seemed to be saying that it had to go deeper than that. It wasn't enough just to look out and see masses of people in need.

Douglas couldn't help laughing softly to himself as he remembered the elderly man who had scolded and challenged him. Because of that he was here, on the other side, and finding out that charity, no matter how well-meaning, could be as cold as winter.

But Cathleen and her grandmother weren't like that. They'd looked at individuals, not cases. He tried to comfort himself with that knowledge.

Chapter Six

It was late. Smoke carrying the scent of wood drifted in the air as Cathleen leaned back against the trunk of a tree and nibbled at a toasted marshmallow. Eyes half-closed, she gazed dreamily into the glowing red coals of what remained of the fire. The only disturbing element to the scene was the soft whimpering of little Kristina, who was growing tired. Even Mary Ann sat close to her mother's side now, her eyes large and dark as she listened to the distant wail of a coyote.

"I think we'd better get these little ones back home," Whit said, getting to his feet. "I'll carry Mary Ann if you'll help Mrs. Marlowe with the baby, Roberto."

Cathleen didn't move as she watched the sudden stirring of those around her. She didn't want this evening to end. She still had a feeling of incompleteness, as though something that was supposed to happen hadn't yet occurred.

Gran had gone up to the house over an hour ago, protesting every step of the way as Whit helped her to the car that was parked just on the other side of the pond. When he came back, Whit had told Cath, "That old lady has enough spark to keep going till midnight."

Cath smiled now, thinking of her grandmother. It was hard to know how much she was well enough to do. Even years of medical experience didn't help her when a member of her own family was involved. She wanted to hold tight, to be particularly careful so as to make sure Gran was safe.

She watched the others get ready to leave. "I'll see to it that the fire is out," she volunteered.

"You can't stay down here alone." Whit frowned at her in big-brotherly fashion.

"I'll take care of it," Douglas told him.

"I'm not afraid," Cath told them both, feeling as though she were being treated like a child. "I'm quite capable of managing alone."

Douglas didn't argue, but she saw the look that he and Whit exchanged. Men! They thought they were being so subtle.

Yet when the others were gone, the darkened area back in the trees seemed a little threatening, the night almost too silent, with only the occasional rustling of small animals, or what she supposed were small animals. Vaguely she remembered some tall tale Whit had told her about a big cat being spotted by the creek about a quarter of a mile from here. A lynx, he'd said. She'd laughed because she'd never heard of any such creatures in this settled area. But now she could imagine glittering eyes looking down on her from the shadows, and she stepped nervously closer to Douglas.

"I'll get some water from the pond to drown the ashes," he said.

"I'll help you." The last thing she wanted was to be left alone while he went even the few feet down to the pond. "We can use the plastic tub that we iced the sodas in."

She started over to where a small amount of melting ice still remained in the little yellow tub, but then she saw a large tumbleweed wedged up against a tree, and forgot her fears at the revival of an old memory. "Watch this," she called. Dragging the tumbleweed over to the dying fire, she pushed it into the coals. After a minute it caught fire and blazed, flames flowing along all the slender threads of the intricate plant like Fourth of July fireworks display. Briefly, the area was lighted and she could see the familiar woods for what they were, not a threatening place at all, and then, too quickly, the light was gone and nothing remained but the faint glow of the coals.

"We used to do that when we were children," she told him, feeling him standing close beside her. She didn't protest when his hands touched her shoulders, then turned her gently around until she was facing him. She wanted this as much as he did, and when he kissed her she responded joyously, feeling that she, like the tumbleweed, was ablaze in every fiber of her body.

They clung for a moment after the kiss, holding tight to each other in the night that pressed against them, then self-consciously stepped apart.

"We'd better put the fire out," Cath said, her voice shaking slightly.

"That may be difficult." His tone was thoughtful, remote, and she felt cut off from him.

She chose to pretend they were both talking about the same thing. She went over and got the little tub, pouring the remaining water on the embers until they sizzled and sputtered, though still glowing red in spots.

He took the tub from her and went down to the edge of the pond, returning with it full of water. "Got my shoes muddy," he said trying to make conversation as he dumped the water on what was left of the fire.

Again it sputtered, but this time the red winked out and only gray ashes and rolling smoke were left as evidence of the fire. In spite of that he went down for another tub of water and, after unloading it on the ashes, stirred them with a stick and shoveled earth over them. "Can't be too careful," he said.

She nodded, then realized that he might not be able to see the motion with no other light than a distant, faded-looking moon.

"Wouldn't want to set the farm on fire," she said. "Gran would never forgive us."

"She's an interesting lady, your grandmother. She talks tough and cynical, but her actions are all kindly. It has been my experience that most people are the other way around."

Cath flashed a grin at him. Anybody who could appreciate Gran had her attention. "She's had a considerable influence on my life. She made me feel that I could do something important, something that counted, if I just tried hard enough."

He stepped toward her, and she fought down an irrational impulse to run. "And that's why you became a nurse?"

She nodded. "That's part of it. But it's more than that. Gran was influential in helping me reach beyond the ordinary world of the hospital to something special, at least to me."

She laughed softly, knowing he'd probably be amused at her ambitions. "Even when I finished nursing school I knew I wanted to be working on the front lines where new strides were being made every day, using state-of-the-art equipment. I was aiming to be one of the best, not just to bolster my ego, but because I wanted to help make a difference in lives that might have been without hope."

"And have you gotten what you wanted?"

It was, she thought, a hard question to answer. "I had to work my way through school and rely on loans and scholarships, and once I finished I thought it would be easy to find my way to what I wanted. But it wasn't, though I certainly learned a lot about people and about different areas of medicine while I was looking."

"Then it was time spent well." He sounded cautious, as though a little uncertain in the face of her determination.

Cath was used to that. "Things began to come into focus one day when I stood in front of the newborn nursery at a little hospital in Oklahoma City. I wasn't there as a nurse. A friend had a new baby and I'd come to see it." She smiled at the memory. "Their daughter was a beautiful infant, healthy and normal. I was admiring her when I happened to look up. A young couple stood just a little down from me. The woman was crying, and the man looked like someone had just punched him in the stomach."

He rubbed at his right earlobe. It was, she was suddenly sure, an unconscious gesture that had become a habit when he was deep in thought.

"They saw me looking at them and the man turned to explain, a little apologetically. He said he was taking his wife home from the hospital, that they'd lost their baby. They left then, walking away as though they couldn't bear to be in that place any longer. I never knew what went wrong, why their baby had died, but suddenly it was more real to me, and I remembered what had originally drawn me into medicine."

He didn't understand, of course; not many people did. Even though they were standing close, the distance between them seemed to increase. She couldn't help feeling a little disappointed; just for an instant she'd thought he might be a person she could talk to, someone who wouldn't laugh at her dreams. But she should have known better, a man like him, a person who knocked about from job to job, must always fight too hard for sheer survival to afford the luxury of being concerned about others.

"We'd better get back to the house," she said, feeling it was time to end what was becoming an uncomfortable interlude. "Or Whit really will come looking for us."

"You talk a lot about Whit McMichaels," he said, sounding tired and irritable. He picked up a sack that contained some leftover cookies and marshmallows in one hand, and the carton of empty soda bottles in the other, while she carried the yellow tub as they strolled up to the dam that led around the pond and back toward the house.

"Whit's my friend." She shrugged. "I'm very fond of him."

"But he's married."

She glanced at him with amusement. It was funny how people like him had one set of standards for themselves and another for women like her. "What does that have to do with anything?"

He didn't answer directly. "What's his wife like?"

"Pretty, not too bright. Not that she's really slow or anything, but she just didn't think things through. If she had, she would never have married Whit."

They walked side by side along the dam, glancing down at the water sparkling below. From somewhere close at hand, Cath heard a frog croak.

"Thought he was such a great guy."

"He is. They just weren't right for each other. Whit loves it out here, can't imagine any other life, and Angie had only the vaguest idea of country life, something based on *Gone With the Wind*, I would imagine. She was going to sit around on the terrace and sip iced tea. Only Whit doesn't have a terrace, just a front porch, and he expected her to be planting a garden, canning, sewing and all the other fun things that his mother had found so satisfying." She laughed, a little bitterly. "I guess you could say they both came into the marriage with some illusions about what the other would be like."

"It's inevitable, I suppose, but couples who really care about each other work those things out."

"Well, Whit cared!"

"You're being defensive about your friend." He sounded annoyed. "Aren't you being unfair to his wife?"

She quickened her pace, walking a little ahead of him. "If you'd ever met Angie, you'd know I was right. She was spoiled and self-centered; she wanted Whit to cater to her the same way her rich parents had, and when he refused to do that, she just took off."

"You sound as though you're taking her defection personally." He tried to help her open the gate, but she hurried to push it ajar without his assistance, slipping hurriedly through and leaving him to follow as best he could.

"Whit is my friend," she reminded him. "Naturally I minded when he was so hurt."

She stalked across the road toward the house, not waiting to see if he was following. Just ahead she could see the van parked in the side yard, Roberto leaning against it, waiting for Douglas.

"It's my opinion that you should consider whether your sympathy played a role in breaking up the marriage." He caught up with her, speaking in a confiding, advising voice.

She glared at him. "I wasn't even here when it happened. I was in Oklahoma City." Furiously, she rushed toward the house, turning only when she reached the step to pointedly wish Roberto, and not Douglas, a good-night. It was only when she was inside and the door closed behind her that the full import of his words finally struck her. Instead of becoming more angry, she burst into soft laughter. He really thought she was part of a triangle involving Whit and Angie! That was really funny, considering all the times she'd listened for hours to Angie's complaints and privately cautioned Whit to use patience with his beautiful wife. Besides, the very idea of Whit's having a romantic role in her life was ludicrous. The relationship between the two of them was about as romantic as...as... She couldn't even think of anything that unromantic.

"What took you so long?" Gran came in, wearing a short cotton nightgown and slippers. Her hair was tousled as though she'd already been to bed. "I saw the others come up ages ago."

"We were just making sure the fire was out." Cath went into the kitchen to put away the leftover food. She tried not to think about the moment when she and Douglas had kissed because she knew from experience that sometimes her grandmother came dangerously close to reading her mind.

"We who?"

"Mr. Boyd and me."

"Mr. Boyd? Thought I heard you calling him Douglas earlier. Next thing I know it'll be Doug."

Cath closed a cabinet door, not looking around at her grandmother. "It'd seem foolish to go around calling Roberto and Douglas by their last names when I'm working with them every day."

"So you just said Mr. Boyd to throw me off the track."

Cath turned to face her grandmother. "Honestly, Gran, you make everything so complicated."

Gran's matriarchal face took on an insulted look. "The last thing I want, Cathleen, is to interfere in your business. You're twenty-five years old and quite grown-up. If you want to throw your life away on the wrong man, I'll be the last person to interfere."

Cath grinned. "I'm tired, Gran, and I don't plan to throw my life away before tomorrow, anyway."

It was funny, she couldn't help thinking, the conclusions people were jumping to tonight: first Douglas thinking she was involved with Whit, and now Gran deciding Douglas himself was the culprit.

"I don't have a thing against the man." Gran's voice followed her as she started toward the living room. "It's not his fault that he's down on his luck."

Thoughtfully, Cath turned to face her grandmother. "I don't so much believe in luck. Oh, I know someone like Sylvia, with her two children to look after, has a rough time. You can tell she's doing everything she can to handle a difficult situation. And Roberto, his family's poor and it can be almost impossible for a member of a minority group to get a decent chance. I admire the way he's out trying his best to get work. But Douglas . . ."

"Douglas is another matter." Gran stated her opinion firmly. "He's obviously intelligent, and he's the kind of person people take to. There can only be one reason why he's living like this. He has no gumption."

"Gumption?" Cath asked doubtfully.

"He's just a drifter, one of those good-looking men who take it for granted that life owes them a living, and so they just float around, sinking lower and lower into the dregs of life."

Cath couldn't help laughing. "That seems a little extreme, Gran."

Gran frowned. "He's not nineteen years old, Cath, not a boy. He's a grown man, and I can't see any reason for his living this way except by choice. There may not be many jobs around here, but there's plenty in other places."

"Come on, Gran, this is hardly any of our business—"

"I just don't want any trouble, and I'm intending to head it off before it gets started."

"What kind of trouble?"

"Trouble. He's not right for you, Cath."

"We just met. We're not exactly the romance of the century yet."

"Just see to it that it stays that way. I'll tell you, Cathleen, it's time you started settling down with some nice man."

"But not Douglas Boyd," Cath said, trying to sound amused.

Her grandmother treated that remark with a look of withering scorn. "Someone like Whit," she said, "stable and dependable."

Cath frowned. "Whit's married, Gran."

"Not anymore. He told me the other day that Angie's getting a divorce."

"Legalities don't change things that much. He's still deeply attached to her in spite of everything."

"He's a practical man. He won't spend too much time mourning a hopeless situation."

"Gran, I'm not in love with Whit. Besides, I have other plans."

"You have a boyfriend back home?"

Cath laughed again. "A girl can have plans that have nothing to do with getting married, Gran." She went over to put an arm around her grandmother. "Come on, let me fix you a cup of cocoa, and then we both need to get to bed."

Mrs. Price nodded absently, but her gaze went to the kitchen window. Cath looked, too, noticing first of all that the van was gone. She wondered if the two men really slept in it.

Then she looked past the driveway to the chicken house where the light from the single overhead bulb burned dimly.

"I had Roberto nail some screening over the windows so the bugs won't get in there," her grandmother said, "but it's a little warm tonight. They might need a fan."

"The breeze felt cool. Besides, where would they plug it in?"

"There's a plug up by the light socket. If you take an extension cord, you can connect it. It may be cool outside, but the air can't circulate well inside a cramped little building like that. It was built for chickens, Cath, not people. I don't see how I can sleep thinking of those children out there all hot and miserable."

Cath smiled. "I'll be glad to take them a fan."

She found a large box fan in the storage room, and Gran located an extension cord.

"Be sure and tell Sylvia to keep the baby away from the cord," her grandmother warned as Cath started out the door with the fan. "Electric cords make dangerous playthings."

"I'll tell her," Cath promised. "And you get to bed, Gran, it's been a long day."

"No, I'll wait for you. There's something I want to give you when you get back."

Cath frowned. "What's that?"

"It's a brooch, has little tiny diamonds in it. Your grandfather gave it to me when we were engaged, so it must be practically an antique by now. You might enjoy wearing it."

"But Gran, I'd enjoy it more seeing you wear it."

Gran shook her head. "No, I always planned to give it to my oldest granddaughter on her wedding day."

"But, Gran, I'm your only granddaughter and I'm not getting married."

"That's why I've decided not to wait any longer."

Chuckling, Cath went out into the night, carrying the heavy fan. That was one thing about Gran, she didn't waste time trying to be subtle.

At the chicken house, she knocked formally at the screen door as though it were any other house. "It's me," she called softly in case the little girls were asleep.

Sylvia came over to unlatch the door and let her in. "Hi." She, too, spoke softly, and when Cath got inside she saw that Kristina and Mary Ann were both asleep on the bed.

"Sorry to bother you at this time of night, but Gran was afraid you would be too warm." She set down the fan and connected it to the plug with the extension cord. "She also said to remind you to be careful of the electric cord around Kristina." She grinned. "Don't mind my grandmother; she wants to mother the world."

"I don't mind," Sylvia whispered. "It's hard for me to understand her. She's been so kind to us. But I must ask a favor of you, as well. I don't have any way of telling time since my watch was pawned. If I'm not out when you start to work, please knock on the door."

"Sure." Cath nodded. "Be glad to."

Sylvia looked relieved. "That takes a load off my mind. I was hoping the sun shining in would awaken me, but it would be so embarrassing if it didn't. And I am tired."

She looked not only tired, Cath thought, but almost sick. The skin under her eyes was darkly shadowed and her face was drawn. "Maybe you should wait a day or two before starting work. Whit wouldn't mind."

"But I would. Soon the cotton will be chopped and I'll have missed a chance to get work."

"Look, Sylvia, I have a little money if you need a loan." The words were spoken impulsively before Cath had time to think. She had very little money indeed. All she'd managed to save after repaying her school loans was a tiny nest egg, in case of trouble. But for Sylvia trouble was already here.

"Thank you, Cathleen, but I would have no way of repaying you."

"Oh, I didn't mean that kind of loan. You wouldn't have to pay me back."

Sylvia smiled, her dark eyes shining with tears. "You're sweet, too, Cath, just like your grandmother."

The compliment embarrassed Cathleen. If only Sylvia knew all the things she'd planned to do with her small hoard of money, then she'd know how hard the offer had been to make. It was the kids, darn it! Who could stand by and let two little girls do without things they needed?

"Don't be silly," she said gruffly. "I'll cash a check tomorrow and get some money for you."

Sylvia touched her arm. "Not yet. We have a place to live and I even have a job for a little. We'll be all right."

Cath looked around. Living in what had been a chicken house and a temporary job chopping cotton didn't seem very "all right" to her. She couldn't help wondering how she'd feel in the same situation. "How old are you, Sylvia?" she asked suddenly, then shook her head apologetically. "I was only wondering if we're about the same age."

"I'm twenty-three."

Cath couldn't help frowning. "But Mary Ann is six already."

"She was born when I was seventeen."

"You must have been married when you were terribly young."

The other girl's face turned beet red, but she met Cath's eyes in a steady gaze. "We hadn't been married long when Mary Ann was born."

"Oh." Embarrassed, Cath felt as though she'd committed some social misstep. How could she be so stupid as to blunder into a situation like this that was awkward for Sylvia, especially when her own work brought her into contact with the realities of life every day?

"I was young. It was a mistake," Sylvia spoke quietly. "Naturally, I can't regret Mary Ann, but I've often thought that if Eric and I had been a little older, gotten off to a better start, things might have been different."

The yearning in her voice stirred Cath's heart.

Chapter Seven

When Cath got back to the house, she found her grandmother in a state of great agitation. "It's gone," she said, clutching at her granddaughter's arm the minute she walked inside. "Everything's gone."

Cath needed only one glance to know that whatever was missing couldn't be as important as her grandmother's well-being. "Settle down, Gran," she said in a soothing voice. "Remember that you've been ill."

"I'm not likely to forget it. And if I did, you'd remind me."

Cath grinned at the snap of her grandmother's tone. "What's wrong?"

"I've been robbed. While we were down at the pond, my jewelry box was taken."

Frowning, Cath took her grandmother by the arm and ushered her into the living room. "Sit down," she said, still trying to be soothing, "and tell me exactly what you're talking about."

Mrs. Price stood firmly in place. "Cathleen, I'm trying to tell you that someone stole my jewelry box while we were out. Just now I went in to find that brooch I told you about, and the entire box was gone."

Cath knew the box her grandmother was talking about well enough, a small lacquered box that she'd owned as long as her granddaughter could remember. As a little girl, she'd occasionally admired its glittering contents.

"But Gran, you didn't have anything really valuable."

"Valuable enough to me. The brooch had diamonds in it... well, tiny ones, of course. But, Cath, your grandfather gave it to me. And there was a lovely opal ring, and some pearls and a few other pieces. None of them worth a great deal, of course." There was no mistaking the look of distress on Mrs. Price's face, and she didn't have to repeat the assertion that, though not of great value, the items were irreplaceable to her.

Cath sank into a chair. "Oh, Gran!"

Gran nodded. "Must mean one of our new acquaintances helped himself."

Cath didn't like the use of the masculine word. "Or herself," she corrected, then realized that only meant Sylvia was included. She didn't like that idea very much either.

Some other reasonable explanation had to be found. "Perhaps you only misplaced it," she suggested.

Gran shook her head. "I always keep it in the top drawer of my dresser and it isn't there. You're welcome to look for yourself if you wish."

Cath got up slowly, feeling as though the effort to get to her feet was more than she could manage. Would this long day never end? It must be close to midnight by now.

She went into her grandmother's bedroom and couldn't avoid her own image in the mirror behind the dresser. She looked awful. Her face pale and her eyes huge with fatigue. The bright-blue striped shirt she'd worn with her jeans only emphasized her pallor. She pulled open the drawer on the right side, the one her grandmother indicated. Nothing was there except some filmy lingerie, as dainty as her grandmother's appearances always was. "You're sure it was here?" she called.

"Quite positive."

She went back into the living room. "Anything else missing?"

Mrs. Price shook her head. "Not that I can think of."

"But, Gran, who would know that you kept your jewelry there?"

"No one, but it's not exactly a difficult hiding place to find. I didn't even lock the house when we went down to the pond. I trusted everyone here." Her voice shook with indignation.

"If the house was unlocked, anyone could have got in." At first the idea made Cath feel better, then she saw her grandmother shake her head and realized the flaw in her theory.

"We would have seen any car that drove up. We have a perfect view from down by the pond."

"That's true. But maybe it was someone on foot."

"Someone walking came up here, went through the house looking for my modest jewelry, ignored the camera and the portable television and ran off down the road?"

It did seem rather implausible.

Gran was seated on the sofa. Cath fell into place next to her. "What do we do next? Call the sheriff's office?"

The silence was so long that she thought she wasn't going to get any reply at all. Then her grandmother finally answered. "Not yet," Gran said, speaking very slowly as though she was extremely tired. "Let's give them a few days. After all, as you said, the jewelry isn't worth that much. I don't want anyone to go to prison over it."

"But, Gran..."

She reached over to pat Cathleen's hand. "What hurts me is that we've tried to help these people and they've turned around and rewarded us by this action. That's how they view life, Cath, as a struggle to see what they can get out of others."

"Oh no, Gran."

"I hope whoever did it may repent and return some of the items—especially when he realizes they aren't really worth a great deal. I'm not optimistic, you understand, but I believe in giving everyone a second chance." She supported herself against the sofa arm as she stood up. "But from now on, Cathleen, we will be more careful. We'll lock the house when we're out, even if we're still on the farm as we were today. And we won't be inviting those...outsiders into our home anymore."

"But, Gran—"

"I mean it, Cath."

Cathleen started to argue, then saw the utter exhaustion on her grandmother's face and refrained. The only thing that mattered was to get her grandmother safely to bed so that she could rest and regain her strength.

After she helped Gran get settled for the night, Cath went to the little room that had been hers during summer visits for as long as she could remember. She undressed slowly, turned out the light and opened the drapes before getting into bed. The evaporative cooler that sent chilled air into the living room, kitchen and Gran's bedroom didn't reach back here. And in spite of the little fan, the room seemed stuffy. She opened the window just above the head of the bed, then lay on her stomach staring out into the night. The stars were brighter now, seeming almost close enough to touch. She wondered if Douglas and Roberto really were sleeping in that old van.

Douglas stirred uneasily, only half awake. What was that awful racket? He sat up, looking across to the other side of the van where the dark-haired young man was buried in a sleeping bag that matched his own, both of them purchased at a Goodwill store. He grinned. The noise was the sound of Roberto snoring, a common occurrence, but one to which he had not become adjusted.

He got up, moving as quietly as possible from the van, and stood out in the cool early-morning air. He was fully awake now, and the wooded pasture area where Whit had given them permission to park seemed particularly lovely in the silvered glow of starlight.

The sight of such lovely things brought his thoughts back to Cathleen, as surely as a homing pigeon nearing its destination. With a quickening heartbeat, he relived the moments when she'd been in his arms, his mouth pressed against hers, and he felt a brief exaltation that she had returned his passion, despite thinking that he was a drifter. But an instant later he had to smile at his own romanticizing. It was as though he were setting up conditions; she had to love him in spite of appearances and then—ta-da! A trumpet fanfare would sound, and he would reveal his true self to her, like the disguised prince in a fairy tale.

Shaking his head, he moved carefully in his bare feet across the rough pasture grass. She wasn't likely to be any more impressed with his real self than with the field-worker. What was he anyway, but a spoiled rich kid who'd had everything handed to him on a silver platter, carefully controlled by the appropriate strings, until not long after his sixteenth birthday, when a near-fatal accident in his new sports car had changed his life?

He'd been moving along a back country road at a speed some twenty miles an hour over the limit when, quite suddenly, a boy on a bike had pedaled out in front of him. He'd hit the brakes even as his brain shouted, "Not enough time," and he'd steered away from the boy and directly into the unyielding side of an old stone bridge.

The boy was untouched; Doug had spent six months in the hospital recovering from his injuries and more time than he'd ever had just thinking. Though Dad and Grandmother had insisted on the best of care, including, of course, the finest private room available, he'd gotten lonely after the first few weeks. The doctor had suggested a roommate.

He was disappointed to be placed in a room with a skinny-looking kid a couple of years younger than himself. It hadn't helped any to be told that the kid had a terminal illness. He'd had a creepy feeling about the whole thing, but before he could ask to be transferred, he and Bob—that was the kid's name—began to get acquainted.

He'd never known anyone like Bob, who had so much sheer joy of life and living. Every day seemed to be an adventure, even in a hospital bed, and fairly soon Doug figured out that he didn't want to be transferred because then he'd miss out on all the fun that always seemed to be going on around Bob.

As naturally as though discussing his enthusiasm for sports, Bob talked of his relationship with God, of his deep faith that carried him through this last, undoubtedly difficult experience of his life. He didn't use the normal religious words, but wasn't exactly offhand either. He sounded almost shy, as though what he talked about was too special, beyond normal speech.

Even now, the memory of those haphazard, apparently aimless, conversations sometimes replayed in his mind, and it was as though he were sixteen again and frustrated and bored to be confined to a hospital bed. He could recall one particular day when it was almost time to go home. Bob had sat on the edge of his bed, painfully thin legs dangling, and grinned challengingly at him.

The broken bones were almost mended now, but time wouldn't hurry enough for Doug. He had no pa-

tience with being sick. "You look as though you're
having a good time," he growled at his roommate.

Bob's grin widened. "And you're not? Wow, that's
really hard to imagine when you've had this long vacation in such a terrific place."

It was an attempt to tease him out of the black
mood and the moments of despair that came so much
less frequently now that he had Bob to keep him company. He sat up enough to punch his pillow into place
more forcefully than was necessary. It was as though
he were taking out all his anger on a poor, defenseless
pillow. And this time he knew why he felt so rotten. It
wasn't so much because he was locked in here while his
friends were gliding through warm spring days. It was
because of Bob. It had taken a while for the informa-
tion to really penetrate his thick skull, but he'd finally
been forced to face the truth that at first had seemed
only so many words. Bob's deteriorating condition
had convinced him of their accuracy. His friend
wouldn't be going home.

"Come on," Bob urged. "Cheer up. We'll see if we
can't talk the nurses into putting us in wheelchairs and
taking us outside so we can see the grass and the
flowers."

"That'd be a nice change. I'm tired of this crummy
building."

"You'll be getting out soon." Bob sounded un-
commonly solemn.

"Sure, I guess so." Doug couldn't help feeling embarrassed. He didn't know what to say. It was hard to
think about incurable illness when you were sixteen,
and even harder to talk about it. "You, too," he
mumbled.

"I'd like to think that." The other boy's thin face took on a wistful expression. "But I don't suppose it'll happen."

"Sure it will," Doug argued angrily. "Don't talk like that."

Suddenly, Bob was himself again, a lively, cheerful teenager. "They've been honest with me, Doug, and I'm glad. It's not what I would have chosen, but I've got to have faith."

"Faith?"

"Sure, I've got to believe that the guy upstairs knows what he's doing." Bob swung his bare feet down to touch the floor, hesitating almost as though contemplating standing, even though they both knew he was too weak. "You know, Boyd, I'm a little worried about you."

"About me?"

Bob nodded. "You've got to wise up. You don't have a good picture of life at all. It's not over when you die, you know. It's just starting. The best part comes after that."

The memory of Bob left a smile on his lips even as the scene from his own mind began to fade. For a moment it had seemed to have more reality than the night around him. He and Bob had gone through a sequence of such conversations, and he'd finally begun to get the message. On the night his friend had died, he came to his own painful acceptance of belief in a power beyond himself.

At first his father and grandmother were tolerant of what they saw as "Douglas on a religious kick." They thought of it as a natural result of his near-brush with death, compounded by the unfortunate attachment he'd developed to that poor dying boy. A few weeks of school and home life, and he'd be back to his usual self.

It didn't happen that way. At first it was simply the only way he could deal with his first personal experience of death. And his own church attending was strengthened by the very fact of his family's opposition. It had been a way of rebelling. But then his convictions began to grow and deepen, to become something that was a unique part of himself. The few weeks lengthened to months, then to three years. When he graduated at nineteen, a year later than his classmates because of the time lost in the hospital, his family was stunned when he announced his intentions to prepare for the ministry.

They opposed him in words and in fact. Funds were cut off. He went from living with every possible luxury to relying on the small legacy his mother had left him.

He altered his plans to attend a prestigious eastern university, instead attending a respected church-sponsored institution in Texas. At first he'd been a little proud of himself, feeling as if he were really giving up a lot to follow God's will. But eventually the truth came down on him hard: his "small" legacy was enough to make him a whole lot more comfortable than most of the other students.

He'd enjoyed the years of study, and when he went home on vacations, he'd tried to ignore the family pressure to take his place in the far-flung business empire that had been established by his grandfather. If there had been other sons or daughters, they might have let him go. But he was his father's only child, and Dad's older sister, and only sibling, had died childless a few years ago. They wouldn't leave him alone.

In spite of that, he'd followed his convictions with single-minded devotion, and after graduation he'd accepted a position as a youth minister in a high-poverty area church. It was there the moment of revelation had come. Could he, with his pampered background, truly serve the kingdom's most needy citizens?

And so he'd come to be here, sleeping in a van in a western Oklahoma pasture, wishing it was morning so that the torment of nighttime thoughts would be ended.

He'd be tired tomorrow. The exhilaration of the cool night air would quickly fade as the sun grew hot, and if he didn't get some sleep, he'd find himself as droopy as a frost-killed plant. He climbed back into bed, wrapping himself in the sleeping bag that felt so good now that the early-morning air was getting cool. Funny how this place could be so hot by day and so cool at night. He looked again at Roberto. How would they manage to sleep in the van after winter set in and the real cold came?

Maybe he'd call it off by then for Roberto's sake. He'd give him his wages for this extended tour of poverty so that he could go home to his girl and get on with his plans for getting some education. And he could go back to his ministry....

As Doug slipped toward sleep, he found his thoughts centered once again on the golden-haired woman who must be asleep by now in the farmhouse just down the road. Cathleen! He imagined her snug in his arms, her mouth against his. Almost angrily, he turned over, moving with difficulty within the confines of his sleeping bag. It would have been better if they'd never kissed, for he didn't want to spend the rest of his life in this sweet torture of reliving the moment and fearing it would never come again. But no! He sat up abruptly.

"Doug, are you all right?" Roberto asked sleepily. "I keep hearing you moving around."

"I'm okay." Douglas lay down again, determined to be still so as not to disturb his friend.

"Can't get her off your mind? I have told you it's not wise, but still it's wonderful to be in love."

Wonderful and terrible, Douglas thought as he closed his eyes and willed himself not to see her face in the darkness. But even so, in spite of everything, he could not sincerely wish that the kiss had never happened.

Morning came quickly and he groaned aloud as Roberto shook him the second time. "Don't want to get up."

"It isn't necessary," Roberto's soft drawl cut through the folds of sleep. "You can sleep late if you like."

Abruptly, he sat up, frowning. "What do you mean I can sleep late? If we don't get to work we'll both be fired."

Roberto shrugged. "This is only a game to you, a sport that you can call off at any minute."

Douglas frowned at the mockery in his friend's voice and yet recognized the truth of what he said. He could never really know how it felt to be this poor, not when all he had to do was go to the nearest phone to tap into virtually unlimited financial resources. He sat, slumped in place, on the tattered old sleeping bag.

"You make me feel like I might as well give up, Roberto."

Alarm came into the dark eyes. "No, my friend." Slowly he shook his head. "It's not the same, and yet you still learn because you care; you feel the pain of those around you. Even if it's close to pretend, you sleep here and you eat when we have food." He paused, seeming to search for words, finally saying, "It matters most that you care enough to try. You seek. You look. It is more than most do."

Still frowning, Douglas got to his feet. He felt angry and out of sorts this morning, probably because of lack of sleep. "You don't have to butter me up, Roberto. I'll tell you right now that even if we quit today, I'll still give you the full sum we agreed upon, so actually you'd gain by my walking out on the whole situation right now."

Roberto stood stiffly, his features rigid. "If you think I am less than honest with you, then perhaps we'd better part company. If you feel that because I'm without wealth I'm also a cheat and a flatterer, then—"

"I'm sorry, Roberto. I didn't mean that at all. It's only my own doubts about myself that are coming through. It doesn't have anything to do with you."

Roberto nodded, and the two men went about getting ready for the day's work, taking advantage of Whit's offer to make use of the facilities of the small bath in the rear of his house in order to clean up.

Douglas found himself reveling in the pleasure of a soapy, hot shower, the first he'd had since they'd spent a night in a commercial camping area a week ago. Abundant hot water was something he'd always taken for granted; never would he do so again.

Afterward, Whit casually invited them to share the breakfast of bacon and eggs he'd made himself. The food smelled so good that Douglas felt his mouth start to water, but he looked questioningly at Roberto.

"Thanks," Roberto said, "but we have food in the van and we don't want to take advantage of your hospitality."

The big man regarded them unblinkingly for a moment. "I made enough for three. Hate to see it go to waste."

Douglas and Roberto looked at each other. This time Douglas was the one who spoke. "Look, Whit, we appreciate your kindness, but—"

"But you're not charity cases. I know that. You're both willing to work hard at whatever I ask you to do, but I know we're a long way from town here and there's no decent housing, so you have to live in that van. You can't cook in a setup like that, and you're going to have a hard time putting in a good day's work without eating right.. So it's to my advantage to see that you're fed." He grinned. "I plan to work you hard today."

Again Douglas looked at Roberto, wondering what his friend would see as the proper code of behavior for this situation. In a flash of insight, he realized how hard it would be to keep self-respect if you were so hungry that the scent of bacon was enough to make you want to sell your integrity.

And they weren't even abnormally hungry, not after two good meals yesterday to make up for a week of cheap makeshift food while they traveled and looked for work.

"Perhaps we can make a deal," Roberto suggested quietly. "You say you do your own cooking, Whit.

Well, I have been told that I cook pretty good. Maybe I can prepare the meals and, in return, Douglas and I will share them with you."

"Sounds good to me," the big man replied cheerfully. "Save me a heap of time, and I can't pretend to be too wild about being my own cook."

The two men nodded at each other with satisfaction, leaving Douglas feeling left out. Was he a child that Roberto, who must be at least eight years younger, had to arrange his meals for him? "I want to do something to pay my way," he insisted.

"How about this morning you get right over to Mrs. Price's place and look after the calves for me?" Whit suggested. "Feed and water them, and then after that, you can do some patching on the roof of the barn where it got blown about in a storm a week ago. And after that, you can meet us in the field to do some more hoeing."

Douglas grinned appreciatively. "Sounds like you plan to keep us busy."

"Sure do. Don't you worry, I'm a practical man and I aim to get value for my money. Now let's sit down and eat before the eggs get cold."

The eggs and bacon and hot buttered biscuits were just about the most delicious food Douglas had ever eaten. He spread one last biscuit with wild honey and considered his own mixed emotions. It was bad enough to have to accept help, no matter how Whit might rationalize it as part of the job, but the worst part was being forced to recognize what a really fine person his rival was.

It would be so much easier if Whit McMichaels were an insensitive, unkind, money-grubbing man. That way Douglas could see himself as saving Cathleen from an unfortunate fate. But this way, well, even he had to admit she'd probably be better off with this stable, kindly farmer than with a man bent on a troubled mission, who had no clear idea what his life would be other than that it would be guided by God.

He left Roberto clearing the farmhouse kitchen and, taking the van, drove the two miles to the other farm. As he fed and watered the calves, he couldn't help glancing now and then at the house, hoping to see Cathleen, fearing to see her. His heart beat faster just at the idea of their proximity, and inwardly he scolded himself for acting like a lovesick teenager.

After caring for the calves, he found the tools Whit had told him to look for in a little utility shed, and he climbed cautiously onto the roof of the barn, ready to do a kind of work he'd never attempted before. It was amazing, he thought ruefully, how enough money could protect a person from ever learning to do anything practical.

After about half an hour's work, he was beginning to feel just a little proud of himself. The patching didn't look too amateurish. He was concentrating so hard on his work that he didn't hear anyone approach and almost fell off the roof when a soft voice startled him.

"Mr. Boyd, can I talk to you a minute?"

He looked down. It was the young mother—what was her name—it took a minute to remember. Oh yes, Sylvia. He climbed down.

Her dark eyes were filled with tears. "I thought I could talk to you," she said.

"What's the problem?" he asked gently, trying not to be anxious about the work he was supposed to be doing for Whit. She did seem genuinely distressed. "Something wrong with your little girls?"

"Oh no. It's early yet, and they're tired from the party last night. They're still asleep. No, it's not Mary Ann or Kristina. They had a lovely day yesterday, the best since their father went away." Tears ran down her cheeks. "I haven't been so good at looking after them by myself."

"I'm sure you've done the best you could. They seem well and healthy." Which was more than could be said for her, he thought privately. Evidently she'd been pushing herself, doing without, to make sure the children had what they needed.

She stared at the ground. "I was so angry and bitter by the time we got here. I swore I'd do whatever was necessary to get by. I'd lie, cheat, steal...."

He didn't know what to say. Once, it would have been easy. He would have told her that hard times were no justification for immoral behavior. But it was difficult to make such a blanket statement when he saw desperation in her face.

"That's why I did it. When she took me into the house, while she was looking for things for us, I went in and took it. I thought 'why did she need so much when my babies didn't have anything. She has a nice house and a farm and people to look after her.'"

Startled, Douglas looked at the little farmhouse. It seemed excessively modest to him, especially when compared to the dwelling where he'd grown up, but he supposed such standards were relative. "Mrs. Price has tried to help you," he pointed out gently.

He could see her swallow as though trying to choke down a lump in her throat. "I know," she whispered.

"But it wasn't her so much. It was the other one, the blond girl."

He frowned. "Cathleen?"

She nodded, still not looking up. "She's got everything: looks, education, a good job. When she gets married, her husband won't want to go off and leave her. He'll feel lucky just to have her."

Douglas wanted to agree fervently with that statement, but refrained, recognizing that the problem at the moment was Sylvia's feelings. "What does Cathleen have to do with this?"

"It was because of her. I was jealous...and tired and almost sick. And they left me alone in the house. They shouldn't have done that."

He shook his head, impatient with the old rationalization. He found it hard to accept the idea that the person who left the keys in the car, the person who left the household door ajar, bore equal guilt for the crime. Was it wrong to trust people, to be just a little unaware of the depravity of others? Or was it wrong, as in this case, to be trying so hard to help that you left your own property exposed?

He found his feelings torn between the distressed woman standing before him and the frightened elderly woman who saw her world changing too much. It was becoming clear that Sylvia had taken something from Mrs. Price's home. "What happened?" he asked, trying to be patient.

She sighed. "I went into the old lady's bedroom, and I went through her dresser. I thought I might find some cash hidden in her lingerie. That's where they hide things, the old ladies. But I found her jewelry box instead. When I opened it, it glittered, and I thought how she didn't need those pretty things, not like my little girls needed something to eat and a place to stay. So I took it and ran outside and put it in my car. Then I went back in and acted as though nothing had happened.''

Douglas regarded her with interest. "So it was successful, then," he said gently.

Her lashes came up and she stared sorrowfully at him. "That was before she started fixing up the chicken house for us, before Cath planned a party for Mary Ann. Late last night the old lady sent her out with a fan because she thought my babies might be hot, and she stayed and talked to me just like . . . just like we were two girls together. She didn't seem to think we were so different from each other."

Douglas couldn't help grinning at her tone. She sounded almost irritated that Cathleen had let her down in this way.

"Anyway, it's more than that. This morning I can see that I don't want my girls to have a thief for a mother."

He nodded, his amusement fading. This was valid reasoning. "So why not take the jewelry back to Cath or her grandmother? I'm sure no more will be said."

"No, no!" She shook her head violently. "I couldn't do that. I'd have to pack up and leave because I could never face them again. And I don't know where we'd go. This is the only thing we've found in ages, and we don't have a dime. Please, you've got to help me."

"What do you want me to do?"

"You could find some way to put it back so that they'd never know it's even been gone. Oh, please, you've just got to help me!"

She sounded close to hysteria. Douglas nodded. "I'll see what I can do." He could probably replace the case without being seen, and if he was, then he'd simply explain privately to Cathleen and Mrs. Price. He was sure they'd understand. But this little family needed help of another kind as well. "You're working too hard, Sylvia. It's a terrible strain for you to carry so much responsibility alone when you're not well."

She looked down. "I'm afraid my husband's not coming back. I have no choice."

"Isn't there someone in your family you could depend on? I'm not certain you're strong enough for this kind of work. What will happen to the girls if you should get sick?"

Her mouth set in a stubborn line. "I appreciate your concern, but I'm not going back home," she said.

Somehow he knew there was no point arguing with her about that. "What about just asking for some assistance then? Most likely your husband would want to contribute to the support of his daughters."

She shook her head. "I don't want to talk about Eric."

Again he sensed the unyielding quality of her refusal. He nodded and got down from the roof. He would help her in the one way he could. "Where is the jewelry case?"

"Still in the backseat of the car, buried under some clothes."

"I'll get it the first chance I have and try to get it back inside."

She grabbed at his arm. "I can't tell you how much I appreciate this."

He couldn't help smiling. "How can you be so certain, Sylvia, that I won't simply take the jewelry and steal it myself?"

Her eyes grew large with shock. Then she shook her head, dismissing the idea. "Anybody can tell you're not that kind of person."

He supposed it was a compliment. He climbed back on the roof, keeping an eye on the house as he worked. When Cathleen came out, dressed in work clothes, he waved to her.

She waved back, but didn't approach or even call out, and he watched, disappointed, as she went over to the chicken house. A little later she, Sylvia and the two little girls headed toward the fields. Mary Ann waved enthusiastically to him as they went by.

"I'll be there to help you soon," he called, "as soon as I finish here."

About thirty minutes later, he was just repairing the last damaged area when Mrs. Price came out of the house. She headed down the driveway, and he watched her thoughtfully. She didn't see him. Good! This was his chance to replace the jewelry box and resolve Sylvia's dilemma without embarrassment.

Climbing down hurriedly, he went over to the old red car and found the box under a tumble of worn-out clothing. He opened it just to make sure the jewelry was still inside and shook his head at what he saw. Poor Sylvia! She'd been willing to turn herself into a thief for such a meager haul as this. The memory of the elegant jewels his own grandmother sometimes wore flashed before his eyes.

No time to waste. He went to the back door, pushing it open. He was uncomfortably aware of his own position as he entered the house. If he were caught, it would be very difficult to explain his presence inside.

He moved quickly through the house, wishing he knew a little more about its layout. But it proved simple enough: a small utility room leading to a kitchen, a dining area, a little living room and then a tiny hall with three bedrooms leading off it. The first one, he felt sure, would be Mrs. Price's.

His heart jumped when he thought he heard a noise. He stood still for several minutes, waiting to hear if someone was coming inside, but the sound wasn't repeated. He yanked open the first drawer, slipped the box inside, closed it and then hurried from the house. Once outside, he was able to breathe more easily, and as he rushed back to put away the tools and join the others in the field, he couldn't help congratulating himself. Obviously he was a man of diverse talents.

Chapter Eight

Cath stayed in place, hidden behind the honeysuckle vine at the corner of the house, unable to believe her eyes. She waited until he'd gone, humming a tune as he went off toward the field, before coming out of cover.

Feeling as though she were trembling all over, she went into the house. "Gran?" she called frantically. "Gran!" It was her first thought, that somehow he'd injured her grandmother. But though she quickly searched the house, Mrs. Price was nowhere to be found, and when she ran to the window, her heart lurched at the sight of her grandmother walking slowly up the driveway toward the house.

At least she was safe. Cath ran out to meet her. "Gran, where have you been?"

Mrs. Price looked as guilty as a small child caught in some forbidden act. "I only took a walk," she said. "A very short walk."

Cath tried to laugh. "You needn't sound so defensive. Walking is good for you as long as you don't overdo it or go out when it's extremely hot."

Reassured, Mrs. Price started toward the house. "That's what tempted me. It's such a lovely, cool morning."

Automatically, Cath responded as she followed her inside. "It won't last. Just give that old sun an hour or two to do his work." People were always talking about the summer heat here. It was a way of life.

"But what are you doing back, dear? You just left."

"Forgot my bonnet," Cath explained, still only half-aware of what she was saying. The picture of Douglas Boyd sneaking—yes, sneaking, that was the only word for it—from the house kept replaying itself in her mind. What had he been doing in here?

She looked around a little frantically, trying to figure out what might be missing. She didn't remember seeing anything in his hands, though she supposed he might have concealed some small object. "Don't see my bonnet anywhere," she said to explain her actions.

"You can use mine. It's in the drawer in my room." Gran headed back toward the bedroom, Cath following.

"You don't keep cash lying around the house, do you, Gran?"

"Cash?" Gran frowned. "What are you talking about, Cath?"

"Well, you said you were going to keep the doors locked, and when I got back from the field just now, you didn't even have the back door closed."

"I knew I would only be gone for a moment and didn't want to bother with locking and unlocking."

"Still, Gran, I think you should check to see if anything's missing."

Gran paused, her hand on the knob of the drawer on the left side of the big, old-fashioned dresser. "Don't be silly, Cath. I wasn't gone long enough for a burglar to get inside. Besides, nobody could have gotten in without one of us seeing him."

But I did see him! Cath didn't know why she couldn't say the thought aloud, why she didn't tell Gran that she'd seen Douglas rushing from the house. Surely there was some logical explanation. She couldn't believe he was a thief.

But why didn't she want to believe it? Her own thoughts were spinning too rapidly. Was it simply because he was attractive and personable? Well, certainly anyone with a rational mind knew that not all criminals were grubby and ugly.

Gran pulled the drawer open, reached inside, then jerked her hand away. "Gracious!"

"What's wrong, Gran?"

Instead of answering, Mrs. Price took something out of the drawer and turned around to hold it out to Cath.

Cath recognized it instantly. "Your jewelry box!"

Mrs. Price nodded. She raised the lid. "Everything's here."

"Are you sure?" Cath's voice was hard. "Check carefully."

They sat down on the bed together, carefully going through the box. Finally, Mrs. Price nodded with satisfaction.

"Every single item is here. Even the costume jewelry."

Cath let a strand of pearls slide through her fingers. "The costume jewelry is the last thing they'd keep."

Gran shook her head. "But why return it?"

Cath looked at the dresser. "Perhaps you just overlooked it before," she suggested without real hope.

Gran got up indignantly to go over and pull open the drawer on the right side. "This is where I kept the box, Cath, and you'll never convince me that I put it in the wrong side by mistake. Not after all these years."

Cath was sure the box hadn't simply been misplaced, but she could tell by her grandmother's defensiveness that the possibility seemed very real to Gran. After a minute, she came back to sit on the bed beside Cath. "Perhaps I could have put it in the wrong drawer," she admitted, "though I don't recall doing so."

Cath patted her hand. "My opinion is that someone took it. What I can't figure out is why he brought it back."

But Gran was already becoming more comfortable with her own theory. "I feel so awful that I blamed those poor people," she said. "I practically accused them of theft."

"Come on, Gran, you didn't say a word to anyone but me."

"But in my mind I said plenty. Why, Cath, I even thought about calling the authorities. How foolish I would have looked when the jewelry box showed up in the wrong drawer."

Cath didn't know what to say. It was unfair to sit in silence like this and allow Gran to put all the blame on herself, and yet she couldn't bring herself to make an accusation against Douglas. He had, after all, apparently regretted his action and brought the box back.

It was unfair to say anything without talking to him first. She would give him a chance to explain before telling her grandmother what she'd seen. Gran was generous, even tolerant, but her ethical standards were inflexible. If she thought he was responsible for the theft, then she'd never trust him again. No doubt she'd see to it that Whit sent him immediately on his way.

Cath contented herself with advising her grandmother, "You might check and make sure nothing else is missing. And after I've helped you do that, then I'd better get back to the field before Whit fires me."

They went through the house from room to room but could find nothing gone. Finally, Cath, having located her own bonnet, got ready to go back to work.

"No more walks until it cools off this evening," she warned her grandmother as she prepared to leave the house.

Gran smiled. "I promise. But, Cath, I'm worried about one thing."

"What's that?"

"You just mentioned how hot it's getting. How are those two little girls going to survive out there all day?"

"They probably won't even notice it's hot. You know how children are."

"I thought you might bring them up here for me to look after. They could nap and rest and have something cool to drink."

Cath placed her hands against her waist, trying to look authoritative. "Grandmother! You are not well enough to try to look after two lively children."

"Just for a little, Cath, so they get a rest from the field."

"I'll think about it," was the most she would promise before leaving the house.

Out in the field, she murmured barely audible greetings to the others, then went to work, trying not to think about what she'd seen. Every once in a while her gaze went to where Douglas seemed to be working in determined concentration.

By noon the baby was crying and little Mary Ann looked hot and tired. Cath was reminded of her grandmother's offer and went over to where Sylvia was filing her hoe.

The other woman eased the file over the blade one last time, then put it down. "Hope Kristina's not bothering you," she said, apologetically. "She always gets a little fretful at this time of day."

Cath glanced at the sun, which now stood overhead. No wonder the poor little thing was cross. Even for adults, the day was hot and miserable. "That's what I wanted to talk to you about. My grandmother told me to ask you to let the girls come in and rest with her during the hot part of the day."

Sylvia's face stiffened. "I couldn't do that."

Cath couldn't help wondering a little dubiously about the kind of pride that allowed two small children to suffer. "You'll be doing her a favor. She gets lonely and bored sitting up at the house by herself."

"Well, Kristina does like to take a long nap, and Mary Ann is never much of a bother."

"Good! Let's take them up there, then." She turned to where the two men stood talking. "If Whit comes by to see how we're doing, tell him we'll be right back."

They nodded, and Cath went over to pick up Kristina, leaving Mary Ann and Sylvia to follow. Mary Ann ran to catch up with her. "Where are we going?"

"Going to have lunch and a nap with my grandmother," Cath explained.

"I don't take naps."

Cath grinned. "I believe you mentioned that yesterday right before you fell asleep."

The child straightened her small shoulders. "Only babies take naps."

"Don't know about that." Cath smiled at Sylvia, who was trudging wearily along just behind them. "I wouldn't mind taking a nap in front of a nice, cool air conditioner right about now."

"Sounds wonderful," Sylvia responded so wistfully that Cath half turned to look at her. Her face was drawn and tired-looking, and she moved as though each step drained her of energy.

"Maybe you should take a rest, too. We can go back to work after the day cools off a little."

Sylvia shook her head. "Mr. McMichaels might think we weren't doing our share."

"Why should he care? He pays by the hour."

"No." The voice was firm. "I need every hour's work I can get."

Cath's reluctance to allow her grandmother to take on the responsibility of the children even for a little while faded when she saw the obvious delight in Gran's face. Maybe what she'd told Sylvia was right and Gran was just plain bored.

"I was hoping you'd come," she told Mary Ann as though she was a much-anticipated adult visitor. "I made a gelatin dessert with bananas and whipped cream."

"That sounds good," Mary Ann said, licking her lips.

"I'll open a can of soup," Cath said, feeling that she was almost more concerned about the mother than the children. She needed to get Sylvia to rest and eat a decent meal. "And I can make some sandwiches."

"No need," Gran said. "I've already got a chicken casserole in the oven. It should be ready any minute now. So all you need to do, Cath, is put together a salad and heat some of those rolls you bought day before yesterday."

"I've got to get back," Sylvia said. "I packed a little lunch. It's still in the field."

"Nonsense," Mrs. Price told her. "You can't run off and leave me when I've already made the food."

Cath was already busily tearing apart lettuce for the salad. "Don't try to argue with her," she advised. "It's impossible."

"Poor browbeaten child," her grandmother commented cheerfully as she took a wet cloth and began to sponge Kristina's flushed face and dirty hands.

"I push Cath around something awful," Gran teased. "At least that's the story she tells."

"It's true." Cath grinned. "My mom is always complaining about how I'm spoiled rotten when I come home from a visit out here. But, Gran, you've got to quit treating me like a kid. I'm twenty-five."

Her grandmother waved one hand in a gesture of dismissal. "Doesn't seem so old to me. Anyway, if you ask me, I'm the one who's been treated like a child lately.''

This wasn't funny any longer. Cath put down the lettuce and hurried over to give her grandmother a quick hug. "Sorry, Gran," she said, her voice husky with tears. "I guess we have pushed you around and tried to tell you what to do. It's only because we've been so worried about you. You gave us a terrible scare."

Her grandmother patted her head as though she were as young as Mary Ann. "You're a rotten child, but I love you, anyway."

Cath went back to her salad-making with a smile. Gran found it hard to express open affection, but she'd always made it very clear how she felt about the people close to her.

When Gran went to take the casserole from the oven, she called over her shoulder to Cath. "I didn't realize I'd made such a huge amount of this. You might as well call the others to come and eat."

Cath stared suspiciously at the casserole. Gran had made this particular dish many times, so she was familiar with its quantity. No doubt she'd doubled the recipe, intending all along to invite the whole crew in. "As long as you don't make a habit of this."

"Of course not. I just happened to have all that chicken and couldn't let it go to waste. It wasn't any trouble at all."

Cath was unconvinced, but she walked back out to the field to invite the men to lunch anyway. Throwing together a casserole that she'd made hundreds of times before probably wouldn't do Gran any harm and having company would perhaps be beneficial. Her reluctance was more tied to her own emotions. She didn't want to deal with Douglas and what she'd seen this morning. Not yet.

She had no choice, though. As she walked across the field, she couldn't help hoping they would have already opened the ice chest with its supply of cold cuts and fruit. But they were standing around talking to Whit, and it didn't look as though any of them had thought of lunch.

"Hi," she called with fake cheeriness. "Gran sent me to invite everyone to lunch."

"Me, too?" Whit asked hopefully.

She tucked her hand around his massive arm. "Especially you."

"We'll just have the sandwiches." Roberto gestured toward the little ice chest that she'd brought out that morning.

"No you won't. Those will keep and Gran's chicken casserole won't. I have strict orders to bring you back."

"If you're sure it won't be too much for your grandmother," Douglas said, smiling pleasantly, as though he hadn't tried to betray them, she thought.

Betray! It was too strong a word. But he had invaded their privacy and taken something that belonged to her grandmother, even though its value was slight. She couldn't help wondering why he'd put it back. Was it because he'd regretted his action, or simply because it wasn't worth enough to keep? Maybe he'd just been afraid of getting caught.

She couldn't bear to look at him. "You two go on ahead," she said. "Whit can help me get the ice chest."

Without another word, the two men started across the field, leaving her alone with their employer. Whit frowned at her, but didn't speak until they were out of hearing range. "What's going on? You sounded mad when you told them to leave just now."

She reached for the chest, but he took it from her, leaving her to walk empty-handed at his side. "Why would I be mad?"

"Can't imagine, but that's how you sounded. Did either of those two do something to offend you?"

She was tempted to tell him. But no, he'd probably fire both of them on the spot. "I'm just hot and tired."

"You don't have to do this, Cath. It was just a joke to start with, and there's no sense keeping it up."

She couldn't help smiling. "And have you say I'm too namby-pamby for fieldwork?"

"Oh, heck! I know better than that. Don't you think I've got sense enough to see that being a nurse is rougher work than this? I don't know how you stand always being around sick people and people who are hurt. I couldn't take seeing a little kid in pain, and I'd faint at the first sight of blood."

She smiled again, patting his arm, and looked up just in time to see Douglas staring back at them. Quickly she dropped her hand, then wondered why she'd reacted in such a way. "I'm glad that Gran is well enough again that I can get out of the house a little and take out my frustrations on a few weeds."

He grinned. "As long as it's good for you." Then the grin faded. "Don't know why I couldn't have fallen for somebody like you, Cath." His voice was gruff with suppressed emotion.

He was thinking about Angie, she knew. "Because I've always been your little sister." Deliberately she kept her tone light. "That's why. We just don't feel romantic about each other and never could, not in a million years."

"I think a whole lot of you, Cath."

"And I of you, Whit. You're probably the best friend I have."

They were approaching the house. Roberto and Douglas had already gone inside, but Whit stopped, holding the ice chest as easily as if it weighed only a few ounces. However, Cath knew how heavy it was, since she'd lugged it to the field early this morning. "I've heard from Angie."

She waited, sure he had more to tell her.

"She's going through with the divorce."

"Oh no, Whit. I'm so sorry."

"Probably for the best. We're not suited for each other."

"But you're in love."

"Doesn't matter. I learned my lesson, Cath. Next time I'm going to make a marriage in the sensible way."

It was a little hard for her to understand how he could be talking about a next union when this one was just beginning to be dissolved. If she'd been in his position, she was sure she'd be so hurt and damaged that she'd only want to run and hide. But, then, perhaps this was his way of dealing with the pain.

"How can you be sensible about falling in love?" she asked wistfully, thinking of the way her own pulse stepped up its pace whenever Douglas Boyd was around. The way she reacted to him was most certainly not sensible.

"It's easy. You pick someone compatible, who feels about things the way you do, somebody you can respect."

Cath thought of all the really nice men she knew, men like Whit whom she genuinely liked and enjoyed spending time with. But they didn't make her heart beat faster just by their mere presence. Couldn't the two go together somehow? Couldn't she be in love and in like at the same time?

"Haven't got to spend much time with you since you got here, Cath. You've been busy looking after your grandmother and I've had piles of work to do, but I thought we might get out and do something together this evening."

"Like what?"

"There's this fancy new restaurant up in town. Everybody says they have good steaks, and they have a guy who plays the organ while you eat."

Cath stared at him. As a teenager she'd gone out with Whit and his group of friends, but they'd never had anything remotely like a date. Which was exactly what this sounded like. "Dinner?"

He nodded. "Sure. I'd enjoy the company. How about I pick you up at seven?"

She started to refuse, then her logical mind told her she was jumping to the wrong conclusion. They were old friends, and he needed someone to listen. Doubtless he'd spend the evening talking about Angie. It would be her chance to put in a few good words for the other woman, explain what it must have been like to come out here and find herself trying to fulfill an entirely unexpected role. She might be able to talk him into giving the marriage a second chance.

She nodded. "I'll be ready."

They went into the house together to find the others already gathered around the long table in the dining room eating the food Mrs. Price had prepared.

Gran looked as though she were having the time of her life, Cath thought, deciding there was no reason to be concerned.

There were two empty places at the table, one between Douglas and Roberto, the other at the end next to Sylvia. Cath started to go sit by Sylvia, reconsidered and took the place between the two men. She couldn't believe Douglas was a thief. She had to find out more about him.

Chapter Nine

In the weeks that followed, Cath alternated between an eagerness to know more about the stranger who had moved into her life and a determination to keep him firmly in his place. She went out with Whit and listened to him talk about Angie, finding her thoughts constantly straying to Douglas. Finally, one Friday, she grew impatient with her own weakness.

She stormed into the house after a morning in the field, grabbed a small bottle of cola from the refrigerator, opened it and took a long swig.

Her grandmother regarded her with interest. "Must have been a rough morning," she said, "if it's driving you to drink."

Cath couldn't help laughing, coming close to choking on her soda in the process. "It wasn't that bad," she admitted, "and I do have the afternoon off at least. Even with as many acres of cotton as Whit farms, he's finally admitted that the fields are virtually free of weeds."

A slight frown wrinkled her grandmother's forehead. "Does that mean Sylvia and the girls will be moving on?"

The thought registered that Gran hadn't even asked about Roberto and Douglas. Gran had become deeply attached to the two little girls and their mother, but Cath couldn't help being aware that it meant all the workers would be moving out of her life. She bit her lip to still the pain that flooded her at the thought. How could she care so much about a man she'd known only a few weeks?

It was like a compulsion that she had to get over. She'd had friends who'd involved themselves in relationships like this, who'd fallen for totally unsuitable men. But she never thought she'd do anything so foolish herself.

"Cath!" Her grandmother interrupted her thoughts. "I asked you if this means that Sylvia, Mary Ann and Kristina will be moving on."

"I don't know, though I suppose so. I did hope, Gran, that you might let them stay on until Sylvia has some sort of definite work lined up."

"It's possible, but they can't keep on living in a chicken house. In another month or so we'll be getting into fall. They can't live out there once it starts getting cold."

"Let's try to buy a little time for them right now. And I'll talk to a few people in town and see if I hear of anything for Sylvia."

Gran shook her head. "That poor girl looks as though the first wind would blow her away. Don't see how she's going to hold down a job until she's built up her strength a little."

"She's managed to chop cotton. That's got to be a lot harder physically than working in a store or office."

"But she's got thinner and thinner. I think she'd be healthy enough if she just had a little time to rest and recover her strength. If only that husband of hers would come back and give her a hand with supporting the girls."

Cath shrugged. "I don't see why she doesn't ask her family for help."

Gran started to say something, hesitated, then began again. "There's some bad feelings there. I don't think she can go back home, Cath. They don't want her."

Cath closed her eyes. Sometimes it was easy to forget that not everyone was fortunate enough to have a close family like hers.

"I'm getting better, Cath. I'd like to see you go on with your plans now."

Her eyes opened wide and she frowned, startled at the sudden change of subject. "What are you talking about, Gran? I have no plans other than staying with you until you're well."

"I am well, or practically, anyway, and I know you must have plans. Girls your age always have plans."

If anyone else had called her a girl, Cath would have argued that she was a grown woman, but from Gran's perspective she had to admit her own youth. "I'm doing fine," she said, "especially now that Whit's cotton is chopped clear of weeds."

Her grandmother's eyes twinkled. "Don't suppose that's all been so bad. You and Whit have sure spent a lot of time together lately. It'd be real nice having my granddaughter settle down on the farm next to me."

Cath stared at her in shock. Finally she found her voice. "Gran, you mustn't plan on that. Nothing like that is likely to happen."

"You can never tell." Gran got to her feet. "I'd better go see if we have some of that grape juice Kristina likes. I want to give you a list to take into town."

"I didn't know I was going into town," Cath said with interest. What was Gran up to now?

"Thought you might get Whit to drive you in, since I need a few groceries. No doubt he could use a woman's help in picking out his own supplies. These bachelors are never much good at that sort of thing."

"My understanding is that Roberto has been doing the cooking and shopping and such. Whit has been bragging about his 'chef.'"

"Can't tell me a man can do a thing like that near as good as a woman."

Cath laughed, going over to give her grandmother a quick kiss on the cheek. "I'll go to town for you, Gran, if you really need some shopping done, but don't think I can't see through your manipulating."

Still chuckling, Cath went to shower and change, feeling almost ridiculously feminine as she put on a crisp pink cotton skirt, a coordinating sleeveless blouse in pastel plaid and white shoes with tiny heels. After days of faded blue jeans and drab shirts, it felt good to dress up a little. She pulled her fair hair up into a girlish ponytail for comfort, enjoying the feel of cool air against her neck.

"I may just treat myself to a fresh limeade at the drugstore the way I used to when I was younger," she told her grandmother as she emerged to take the shopping list from her.

Mrs. Price's smile was only a little smug. "I called Whit. He'll be by for you in about five minutes."

"Gran!"

"Had no intention of calling him, did you? Planned to drive in by yourself."

"I can drive a car," Cath disgustedly informed her grandmother.

"But it'll be more fun to go with Whit." Gran settled herself onto the sofa, turning the remote control to her favorite afternoon television serial. She looked as comfortable as a kitten on a soft cushion, and Cath knew she was entirely pleased with herself.

She shook her head, knowing there was nothing she could do about it now that Gran had already arranged everything. Not that she minded having Whit's company on the twenty-mile drive, but she couldn't be happy about Gran's assumption that there were budding romantic possibilities between them. It simply wasn't true.

She watched out the window until she saw Whit's pickup pull up the driveway. "Here he is now, Gran. I'm leaving."

As Cath left the house, she waved to Mary Ann, who was just emerging from the chicken house. "I'll bring you a treat from town," she called, feeling almost as though she were going on a holiday after the long days of work. She ran to the pickup, not giving Whit a chance to get out but opening the door herself. But then she saw that the driver was Douglas, not Whit, and stood staring at him.

"Whit had to go help a neighbor with a sick horse," Douglas told her. "He sent me in his place. Hope you don't mind."

She was tempted to turn and run. She didn't want to spend the afternoon driving into town with Douglas, she told herself as she climbed in beside him. "I can drive myself. There's no need for you to go."

"But there is," he assured her earnestly. "Whit asked me to pick up a part for one of the tractors."

So much for Gran's idea about a big romance between her granddaughter and Whit McMichaels! Cath almost giggled at the thought that being married to Whit would be like this. He would always be more concerned with his farm equipment and sick animals than with her.

"Hope you don't mind the substitution." Doug sounded as though he was sure she did mind.

"No, it's not that," she answered, her mind focusing on something other than the conversation. For a woman who always thought of herself as having a good grip on reality, she certainly became scatterbrained when she was in his company. It had to be chemical, she decided, some sort of trick of nature. They had no shared interest, no common meeting ground.

She sat quietly while he backed the pickup so that they could move down the driveway, then looked steadily out her window at the fields where the sizzling August heat seemed to waver like a visible force.

"Could use a good rain."

She nodded. "We got a lot of moisture in the spring when my parents were here, but we've hardly gotten more than a sprinkle since I came to stay with Gran."

"Whit spends a good deal of time staring optimistically up at the clouds."

"Well, you have to be an optimist to be a farmer." She turned to smile at him. "It's such a gamble."

He nodded. "I've always thought that was why people who work the land stay so close to God. They know they can't control the forces that make their work a success or failure. They can't make it rain...."

"Or keep the insects away or control the hail and wind that can destroy a crop."

He smiled. "It would certainly help to make you conscious of the value of prayer."

"I learned my belief in God from Gran when I was too small to understand half of what she was trying to tell me, but I could look around at this vast land and find it easy to accept the idea of a force greater than myself. And Gran talks about cosmic matters as though they were as ordinary as...as a cow giving birth down in the pasture."

"But that's a miracle, too."

"I suppose. There's a whole bunch of things in life that we take for granted, from the sun coming up in the morning to its going down at night. These things are quite remarkable, but we find a lot of reasons for everything that happens; we don't give God credit for many things."

He smiled at her. "All the everyday miracles."

She nodded. It was a phrase she liked. Right now it seemed particularly appropriate because, in spite of all the logical arguments going through her mind these past few days, the way she felt sitting at his side at this moment was a kind of miracle, too. The air inside the pickup seemed to sparkle with some heightened degree of sunlight, and she felt more vibrantly alive than she ever had before.

Right now it seemed that they shared a common view of life, a passionate intensity that made each want to reach past the ordinary to live for a purpose beyond the average life-style. It was, she supposed, the reason she'd become a nurse. She had to have work that really meant something. And the way he'd just spoken, she could almost believe he felt that way, too.

She swallowed hard, feeling a happiness rising in her throat. Today she would forget all the problems and just enjoy being with him. Tomorrow would be another matter, and she would have to face reality, but just for a little while she would pretend that he was one of the men like Whit, whom she'd known all her life and could trust. Inadvertently the picture of him rushing from the house came into her mind, and she tried to dispel the thought. "What do you think of our part of the country, Douglas?" she asked, just to keep the conversation going.

"I like it," he said, "though it was hard at first to get used to the open spaces. I missed the woods."

"People around here say that trees spoil the view." It was easy to laugh this afternoon because she was so happy. "We do have some woods," she told him. "Stretches along the creeks where there's enough moisture to help trees grow. In fact, there's a spot not far from here."

"I'd like to see trees," he said a little wistfully.

She leaned impulsively forward, pointing. "Turn to the right at the next corner. We'll take a little detour."

He turned as indicated and they found themselves on a graveled road that seemed to get worse every quarter mile. Soon they were jostling along a narrow lane pitted with holes, but as she'd promised, trees lined the sides of the road. They entered an area where huge old cottonwoods and oaks leaned out to lap branches above them. The road was no more than a single sandy lane.

"This is the local lover's lane," Cathleen explained.

He glanced wickedly at her. "Seems a shame to let it go to waste."

"Only meant for use in the evening hours," she assured him demurely. "Anyway, this kind of thing is for kids."

He slowed the pickup to a crawl, then drove over onto the edge of the road, a narrow ribbon of grass that didn't provide enough room for safe parking.

She turned around to look back. "What are you doing? Nobody can get past us here."

"Doesn't look like we're going to be caught in a traffic jam." He moved decisively toward her, encircling her shoulders with his arm, and pulling her against him. He turned her to face him so that when he held her close the strength of his chest embraced her softness. She looked up at him, forgetting everything but the gentle lilt of birdsong. She lifted her mouth to his, seeking... and closed her eyes as his lips touched hers, sending warmth throughout her body, seeming to melt her bones. Shakily, she opened her eyes to splashes of light, the sun glittering through the leaves above the pickup, and she smiled at him. "I told you this place was for the local teens."

"I'm sure they won't mind if we borrow it for just a little while." He touched her forehead, brushing back a strand of hair that had fallen into her eyes.

It was an infinitely simple gesture and yet she shivered, abruptly aware of reactions that had only simmered beneath the surface before. Blindly she reached up again to meet his kiss. She didn't care what he was or who he was. All that mattered was that he could make her feel as though all the world was singing around them.

"Cathleen, dearest, there's something I want to talk to you about." He nibbled at her chin, then gently nipped the lobe of one ear.

"What's that?" she whispered back. Somewhere out there was a real world with problems that needed answering, but she didn't want to think about that. She wanted to run her fingers over his wrist and up his arm, feeling the texture of weathered skin. She wanted to kiss him again.

He obliged, then pulled only inches away, laughing shakily. "How can I explain anything to you when you're like this?" He reached out to touch the tip of her nose with one finger. "Not that I'm complaining."

She rested her head against his shoulder. "Go ahead, explain whatever you like."

She felt his chest heave as he took in a deep breath, and she could hear the thud of his heart. He seemed to have forgotten what it was that he'd wanted to say. "You were going to tell me something," she reminded him.

"It must be great out here at night. Even at the farm the stars seem to stretch across the skies forever. There's a feeling of infinity."

She liked his description and was dreamily considering it when a horn honked behind them. Startled, she sat up abruptly.

She slid away from him and sank down in her seat, amused and embarrassed. "Get us out of here, please. And don't tell me that's someone I know back there."

He started the motor, then turned to give a little wave to the driver behind them. "A boy," he told her. "Looks to be about sixteen or seventeen. He's in a big car, too big to turn around on this country road, and he's grinning broadly so I guess he's not too upset."

"He thinks it's funny," Cathleen said grimly. "I wonder how long he sat back there."

"Not long, I'm sure. Anyway, you'll probably never see him again." Douglas smiled as though he thought the whole thing was funny, too. After they'd turned the corner and headed back toward the road, he glanced at her. "You can surface for air now. He went in the other direction."

She straightened, but looked around guiltily. "Everybody knows Whit's pickup," she said.

He grinned engagingly at her, looking like a boy who'd enjoyed every minute of his misbehavior, but this time she couldn't smile back. It was as though she'd left a make-believe world behind on that narrow, shady road, and now was coming back to reality.

"You said you had something to tell me," she repeated quietly as they moved back onto the highway.

He nodded, his expression suddenly solemn. "I wanted to tell you that I'm not exactly what I seem."

She stared ahead. "I guessed that."

He seemed strangely reluctant to continue. "I-haven't been a farm worker for long. In fact, this was my first real experience in the fields."

"You didn't have to tell me that. It was fairly obvious that you didn't know a cotton plant from a corn stalk."

He glanced reproachfully at her, obviously offended. "Come now, I'm not that much of a novice."

She couldn't help smiling. "If you're trying to tell me that you're one of those people who decided just to take off and bum around the world, then I might as well admit I already knew. And I want you to know that I think it's a dirty trick to take work away from people like Roberto and Sylvia who really need it." The words were not the ones she'd intended. They sounded so harsh and unsympathetic. "I guess you'll be going away now that the chopping's finished."

"Not right away. Whit says he's got more work for us. I'm to start doing some plowing tomorrow, something to do with the wheat crop."

"I don't know why you'd want to bother!" Cath didn't know why she was so startled; it had been perfectly evident that Whit was more than pleased with the two strangers he'd hired. But then Whit didn't know what she did. He hadn't caught Douglas sneaking off from her grandmother's house.

It hadn't seemed a problem before, but now Whit was trusting Douglas with valuable equipment. She well knew that the big tractor had cost more than some people's homes and that other equally expensive farm machinery made up the inventory for Whit's business. She would have to warn him.

"What's wrong, Cathleen? Are you ill?"

"Why do you ask?" Her lips felt so stiff and wooden that she could barely get the words out. The sunshine of the day seemed dimmed.

"Your face suddenly went pale."

She did feel sick, but knew it wasn't from any illness. The thought of having to go to Whit and tell what she knew made her nauseous. She looked at Doug, at the concerned blue eyes and intelligent face.

It couldn't be. There was some kind of mistake. This man wasn't a petty thief who would sneak into someone's home and take their small treasures. She drew in a deep breath. "I'm feeling better already."

"Are you sure? Perhaps you should see a doctor."

Laughing, she shook her head. "I'm tired and I've had a little too much sun these last few days, that's all. I need to prescribe a few hours' change of pace for myself. Doing the shopping for Gran and Whit's errands will fix me up."

He frowned thoughtfully. "Doesn't sound like much of a vacation to me. Have you had lunch?"

"No, but..."

"Then you'll have to eat with me. We'll find a restaurant and splurge. That way we can really have a chance to talk."

She didn't like the idea of spending his hard-earned money in such a casual way. Maybe it was this carefree attitude that had landed him in such desperate straits that he'd needed the job at the farm. "I'm not sure we'll have time for lunch," she said, hedging.

"A sandwich, anyway. That won't take long."

Wouldn't be too expensive either. Cathleen smiled. "I know a place that makes terrific hot steak sandwiches."

"Sounds great."

She directed him to the modest-looking restaurant out on the highway that led through the north edge of town. In spite of its appearance, it was the place where most of the local people stopped to eat, knowing they could depend on the food to be excellent.

It wasn't until they were out of the pickup and headed inside that Cath remembered that she'd be likely to meet friends of her grandmother as well as her own companions from previous summers. Everybody stopped at the Flamingo, even if only for a piece of pie and a cup of coffee.

"What's wrong?" Douglas frowned down at her.

She could hardly tell him that her presence here with one of Whit's temporary workers was bound to cause comment. Not that she minded, but some people could be too blunt. She hoped he wouldn't be caused any embarrassment.

She drew a breath of relief as she quickly scanned the diners. No familiar faces. Good!

But the relief was short-lived. They'd barely gotten seated and were looking at the menus when a plump middle-aged woman, followed by a skinny man in western clothing, entered the restaurant. "The Martins!"

"Someone you know?"

"Friends of my grandmother. They live on a farm about five miles from hers, and they've known each other for years."

"You don't sound pleased to see them."

She grinned, peering over her menu. "Don't know why you'd say that unless it's because I'm trying to use this menu to hide behind."

He leaned closer to whisper, "Just exactly what's wrong with the Martins?"

"Nothing really; it's just that I never know how to take Mrs. Martin. She's very outspoken and opinionated."

"Well, you might as well quit hiding because they've spotted you, and they're headed this way."

"Cathleen!" Mrs. Martin was several feet in front of her husband and greeted her with open enthusiasm. Mr. Martin was less emotional, but his slow smile showed genuine warmth, and Cath couldn't help feeling guilty for wanting to avoid them.

"How is your grandmother?"

"Much better, thank you, Mrs. Martin."

"It was good to see her back in the club last week."

"We both enjoyed being able to attend, but she wasn't able to get out until recently."

"You could have come by yourself even if Harriet wasn't up to it."

Cath told herself she'd never get used to Peggy Martin's directness, not even if she lived next door to her for the rest of her life. The best way she knew how to respond was to be just as direct. "No, I couldn't. Up until the last few weeks, she wasn't well enough for me to go without her. I still don't like to leave her at the farm alone."

Mrs. Martin pursed her lips. "But you're here." She looked around as though expecting to see her friend hiding under the table.

"But she's not alone now."

"We heard Harriet had taken in some renters." Mr. Martin spoke for the first time, his slow drawl an abrupt contrast to his wife's rapid speech.

"In the chicken house!" Mrs. Martin added. "What kind of people would live in a chicken house?"

"A young woman and her two small children," Cath retorted sharply, "who have nowhere else to stay."

Mrs. Martin frowned. "Well, I can't imagine putting myself in that position. Anyhow, Cathleen, you haven't introduced me to your friend."

Cath blinked at the abrupt change of subject, then glanced at Douglas. The look in his eyes told her he was enjoying the discussion immensely.

"I'm Douglas Boyd," he said, introducing himself. He and Mr. Martin shook hands, but Mrs. Martin regarded him suspiciously.

"Don't believe I've seen you around here before. You must be one of Cathleen's friends from the city."

Cath would have been content to leave the matter right there, but Douglas shook his head. "No, I'm working for Whit McMichaels."

The Martins exchanged glances. "We heard he hired some strangers," Mr. Martin said in his slow voice.

"Taking quite a chance if you ask me," Mrs. Martin added.

"Now, Peg," her husband cautioned gently.

She leaned toward the two seated at the table. "It's not that I've got a thing against you, young man, but we've had a bad time around here lately. Our place was burglarized while Jeff was out of town and I was at the doctor's one day."

"That was before Douglas and Roberto got here, so they wouldn't have heard about it," Cath added quickly.

"Well, it was just the start. We've had a couple more houses broken into since then. It's been a regular epidemic."

Cath stirred uneasily. "I hadn't heard that."

"It's been really bad," Mrs. Martin went on. "Your grandmother has been lucky that her house hasn't been hit. What scares me is that whoever's doing it is going to break in one day when someone's at home and somebody'll get hurt.''

"I hope not," Cath whispered, her mind on automatic. Again she was seeing Douglas sneaking off from Gran's house. The Martin burglary had happened only a few days before he and Roberto had come to Gran's farm. Maybe they'd already been in the community. She felt sick again.

The waitress came to take their orders, and the Martins had no choice but to find their way to a table of their own. But Mrs. Martin reached over to pat Cath's hand. "I'm real glad you were able to come out and look after your grandmother. It's meant a lot to her. She thinks the sun just about rises and sets on you, and I've got to admit that not many young people these days would give up their own plans to spend the summer with an old woman."

Peggy Martin started away, then turned around. "And you might tell that girl who's living in your chicken house that we've got a clothes closet and a food closet up at the church, and she's welcome to come and take what she needs." She hesitated only an instant before glancing toward Douglas. "That goes for you and your friend, too, young man. We wouldn't want anybody to go without."

Cath couldn't help laughing a little at the look on his face. She bent close to whisper. "In spite of everything, she's the kindest person imaginable."

"I can see that, but I'm not used to being an object of charity."

Cath's expression became serious. He lived in a van and did whatever temporary work was available, and yet he talked as though he were used to a different lifestyle.

"What'll it be?" the waitress asked impatiently. "Or would you rather have a little more time to make up your minds?"

"I think we both want steak sandwiches," Douglas told her, glancing at Cathleen for confirmation. When she nodded, he went on to order salads and iced tea.

Cath barely listened. Her attention had been attracted by a small group that had just come in the door. She recognized the hefty man in uniform as the local chief of police, but the others accompanying him were unfamiliar. A tall, silver-haired man looked over the diners much as she had upon entering, seeming to search for someone. Then he looked straight at the table where she sat with Douglas. His eyes widened, and he said something in a low voice to the police chief.

"That man acted as though he recognized us," she whispered to Douglas, whose back was to the door.

He turned slightly, a look of consternation coming to his face. The small group, led by the tall silver-haired man, was headed in their direction.

Chapter Ten

So the moment of reckoning had come! Douglas was fully aware of the slight stiffening in Cath's posture and wished he had time to explain. No telling what she was going to think of him now.

It seemed that everyone in the restaurant was watching, their attention captured by the uniformed policeman. But Douglas had no question about who was actually in charge of the group. Steven Boyd had a natural air of authority, whether it was in the boardrooms of large corporations, or in his personal life. No one knew better than his son.

Even after the silver-haired man arrived at their table, he didn't speak for a moment.

Douglas sat quietly, realizing that he was expected to stammer greetings and apologies like a runaway child. He didn't even bother to wonder how his father had found him. It was easy enough when resources were unlimited. But Dad was going to find that the years had made some changes in the uncertain, idealistic boy who had left home. He waited, forcing the other man to speak first.

The waitress edged in between the men to place glasses of iced tea and plates of salads on the table, then moved away.

"Hello, Douglas," his father finally said.

"Hello," Douglas replied.

Douglas wasn't sure what he felt at the sound of the familiar voice—certainly not the kind of pleasure most men would have felt at seeing a parent for the first time in years; he and his dad didn't have that kind of relationship. There had never been time for love or even friendship to develop through the years in which Steven Boyd had been a mover in the world of business. In fact, Douglas had spent more time in the care of hired attendants—and then away at school—than he ever had with his own family. No, he analyzed now, what he felt was the faintest tremor of fear that this man, who had so powerful a personality, could make him into something he didn't want to be.

"You're a hard man to find," his father said.

Douglas looked at the other men behind his dad. "I see that you had to resort to the help of the police."

"I could hardly just give you a call when I didn't have any idea where you were." Mr. Boyd turned to look at his assistants. "Thanks very much for your help, but I can handle this from now on."

The men nodded and turned to leave.

Steven Boyd directed his attention to Cathleen, but spoke pointedly to his son. "If your friend will pardon us, then I think we have some private matters to discuss."

Douglas felt his face grow warm with anger. This was so like his dad to dismiss his friends as insignificant.

"Cathleen and I were just about to have lunch."

She reached across to touch his hand. "It's all right. I'm not very hungry. I'll go do the shopping for Gran and then come back for you."

He wanted to stop her, but, glancing at the set, impassive face of his father, he knew he didn't want her exposed to what was bound to come in the next few minutes. "That might be best, Cathleen," he agreed quietly. He wouldn't introduce her to his father. After barging in this way, Dad didn't even deserve that courtesy. "I'll see you later."

She nodded, looking worried. "I know a good lawyer if you need one, Douglas."

The suggestion startled him, but then he smiled. "Thanks, Cathleen, I'll keep that in mind."

He watched her go, entranced as always by the look of her, but even more now by the essence, the essential being that was Cathleen. Roberto had been wrong. She was learning to care for him in spite of everything. He was almost sure of it.

"I've come a long way to see you." Steven Boyd's deep voice cut impatiently into his thoughts.

Douglas looked at him. "I'm going to marry her," he said.

Steven glanced around at the door through which Cathleen had just departed. It was as though he hadn't noticed her before now and wanted to see what she looked like. "She's pretty enough, I suppose, but will she fit into your life-style?"

Douglas smiled. "I think she'll fit just perfectly. Now all I have to do is convince her."

His father shrugged impatiently. "Any girl would jump at the chance to marry you."

"You mean to marry the Boyd fortune and power. But Cathleen isn't like that. Anyway, she doesn't know."

"We have more important things to talk about right now."

Douglas couldn't think of many things more important to him than the woman he hoped to marry, but he waited without saying so. That first edge of fear, the feeling of being a boy again, had vanished. Now he was in control of himself.

"Enough of this game playing," his father said. "It's time you came home and took over your responsibilities."

The waitress came, depositing steak sandwiches in front of them. "If you want something else, sir..." she said, looking at Mr. Boyd.

"This will be fine." He waved her away. "You're almost thirty-years old, Doug. It's time you grew up."

Thoughtfully, Douglas took a sip of iced tea. "I am an adult, Dad; my way of growing up was different from yours."

"This religion nonsense!"

"I'm a minister, Dad; it's my profession and my calling. That will never change."

This had all been said before many times and with infinitely more words in shouting matches as well as low, intense conversations.

Mr. Boyd sighed. "Look, Son, you know I have as many religious convictions as the next person, and I can understand that you want to do something meaningful with your life. But this notion of being a minister is something else. I'm almost beginning to believe you're going to stick by it."

Douglas nodded. "You can believe it, Dad."

His father closed his eyes. "If I admit that, then I give up everything. It's over."

"How can you say that?"

For one of the first times in his life, his father looked straight at him and really seemed to see him. "I'm getting older, Doug. What have I built my businesses for if not for my only son?"

"You continue to hope for this even after all these years. You're serious?"

"Serious enough. Nobody's said I'm going to die tomorrow or anything like that, but it makes a man think of his own mortality to see the birthdays creeping past him."

"And his immortality?"

"You don't have to preach a sermon to me. I'm not against these religious beliefs of yours, though they've never had the reality for me that they do for you, but in a way I've always felt that you're my immortality. That's why a man has sons."

Douglas knew there was no use arguing. In spite of their distant relationship, he couldn't help being stirred by this announcement of his father's. Somehow he'd always pictured Steven Boyd as going on forever. "How's Grandmother?"

"Fine. She'll probably live to be a hundred. She wants you to come back, too."

He couldn't help thinking about Cathleen and her relationship with her grandmother. A lot of years had passed since he left home; maybe it was time he tried again to forge closer relationships. "I'd like to see her."

"We can drive to Oklahoma City right now, catch a plane and be home by the end of the day."

Gently he shook his head. "No, Dad. I'll be glad to visit, but my life is here right now."

"Doing what? My detectives tell me you aren't even working in a church?"

Douglas ignored the hint of sarcasm in his father's voice. "I'm going through an experience now that's designed to make me better able to work inside the church."

"Doesn't make sense to me."

He didn't want to explain, being quite sure his father would fail to understand his motives, but he owed him that at least.

He told him about his experiences in the church in San Antonio, and about how advice from his elderly friend had led him from oil field to cotton patch, and he was surprised that his father seemed to be listening with a kind of puzzled attentiveness.

Afterward, he stared down at the food cooling on his plate, waiting for the derisive comments he was sure would come.

Finally, Steven Boyd spoke. "It's not a fair test," he said. "You're not really poor, so you can't ever know exactly how those others feel. Underneath, you wouldn't ever be able to forget that it wasn't real, that one phone call would get you out of any situation."

Douglas nodded. "I have a good friend who pointed that out, but I have learned to care about the people around me, Dad, and their suffering is entirely real. I hope I'm a different person from the one who started out on this quest. I hope I'm less judgmental and a whole lot more understanding."

"And you've gone without, been hungry and tired and dirty when you didn't have to be any of those things, just to try to have more empathy with those in need?"

"That's right."

Mr. Boyd rubbed his forehead. "I'll never understand you, Son, but I'm proud of you just the same."

It was the last thing Douglas had ever expected to hear from his father. Maybe the years they'd been apart had changed both of them.

"Then you do see that I can't do what you want?"

"I'll never accept that." This was the old Steven Boyd again, the indecisiveness and pain gone from his voice. "It's your duty to take over the management of the family businesses now that I can no longer do it."

"It's not possible, Dad. I have my own life to lead."

"You'd simply turn your back on everything that's mattered to your family?"

It was an impossible situation to debate. His father would never understand. "Perhaps someday I'll have a son or daughter who'll inherit your talents," he suggested gently.

To his surprise, his father cracked a wintry smile. "I might just stick around to see that day."

It was the first time in a long while that they'd smiled at each other. Douglas found himself enjoying it. "I have a feeling you will."

The waitress deposited the check on the table and Steven reached across to take it. "I'll pay this. You probably don't have enough money in the pockets of those disreputable-looking old jeans to take care of it."

Douglas didn't argue. It seemed only fair to let his dad take care of the bill since neither he nor Cathleen had gotten to eat a bite of the food anyway. As they walked toward the front of the restaurant, the older man stepped close to whisper. "You needn't think I'm giving up this easily."

Douglas laughed. "No, Dad, I'd never deceive myself that way."

"I've got a room here in town and I'll be around for a while. I'll be seeing you again."

Douglas nodded.

After the check was paid, they went outside together. "I have a rental car. Can I drop you someplace?"

"We'll just have to look for the closest grocery store. I want to find Cathleen and help her do the shopping for her grandmother."

"Sounds like an exciting way to spend an afternoon," his father commented cynically.

"Oh, it gets better. After that we have to pick up a tractor part."

"I'll bet you can hardly bear the excitement."

Douglas laughed. "If you only knew, Dad. Being with her is the most exciting thing in the world."

His father's face suddenly took on a serious look. "You sound as though you're really in love with her."

Douglas reached out almost convulsively to grab the door handle of the expensive-looking automobile to which his father had directed him. "I am," he said, and the words were both a promise and a prayer.

Chapter Eleven

Cathleen's hands were shaking as she put grocery items into her cart. She stared at the list Gran had given her, barely able to make out the next word.

Coffee. Gran liked a particular brand. Cath searched the display for it. There it was. She put it in the cart.

Inside she felt like crying, but she was dry-eyed and not just because there were too many shoppers around who would see her in tears and stop to inquire what was wrong. It was more than that. This hurt was too great to be soothed by weeping.

She was halfway down an aisle, looking for a brand of cookies that Gran liked to get for Mary Ann and Kristina, when she saw Peggy Martin just ahead. How had the Martins gotten through their meal at the restaurant so quickly? She looked down at her own nearly full cart. It had taken her a while to collect all those groceries.

She wanted to duck, to run and hide, but there was no escaping her grandmother's friend, who approached with a smile.

"Fancy running into you again. It's a small world."

Cath tried to smile. "And a small town," she croaked.

"Sure is. Your friend was still over at the restaurant talking to that silver-haired man when we left. Jeff had to do some errands, so he left me to do the shopping by myself. Men don't have much patience when it comes to buying groceries, though they sure can eat them."

"Douglas was still talking with the man at the restaurant?" Cath asked, trying to sound as though she were just making conversation.

"Sure was. You could have knocked me over with a feather when the police chief and those other fellows came waltzing up to your table. I wanted to rush right over and find out what was happening, afraid something was wrong with your grandmother, you see. But Jeff made me stay right where I was. Said it was none of my business. And he was right. In a minute I could see that it was your friend they were after."

"They did want to talk to Douglas," Cathleen admitted cautiously.

Mrs. Martin shook her head. "You and Harriet have got to be more careful. Can't just go taking in every Tom, Dick and Harry that comes along. Now that you've gotten rid of this one, I hope you've learned your lesson."

"Gotten rid of him?"

"I'm sure the police will see that he leaves town—if they don't lock him up." Mrs. Martin glanced at her watch. "Oh, I could stay here talking to you all day, but I've got to hurry. Jeff will be back and waiting for me."

Cath was not sorry to see her go. Her hands were shaking more than ever, and her vision blurred as she tried to read the list. She would not cry! But tears filled her eyes in spite of her resolve.

No use even trying to finish the shopping. Wheeling her cart toward the front, she chose the shortest line and waited to check out the groceries, wishing she could run out of the store instead and rush home to the comfort of familiar surroundings.

But she couldn't do that. She had to go back for Douglas. And what if Peggy Martin was right and he wasn't there? What would she do next? Should she call the police station, search the local jail? Or would he have simply left town without further word, vanishing as suddenly as he'd come into her life?

She'd have to tell Roberto, explain to him that his friend had gone. And the others—Whit, who had come to trust him even with his valuable equipment; and Gran and the little girls. It would be the hardest task she'd ever done.

She was just writing a check to pay for the groceries when she felt a hand on her arm and looked up to see Douglas standing at her side.

She was speechless with sudden anger. After all the worrying she'd been doing, here he stood looking as though nothing was wrong.

"Thought I'd save you a trip back to the restaurant, so I had my friend drop me by here."

"How did you know where I was?" She handed the check to the clerk.

"It was the second grocery store we checked. I saw Whit's pickup out in the parking lot."

She nodded, trying to hold on to her poise at least until they got out of the store. He took the cart from her, refusing assistance from the boy who offered it, and pushed it outside. Cathleen followed, feeling as though she were trapped in a nightmare.

She stood by helplessly while he loaded the groceries into the back of the pickup. "Hope you didn't get anything that'll melt. We do still have to stop by the tractor place."

She shook her head. "I didn't get to the freezer case, but I think I got enough to get by until we come into town again."

Once everything was loaded, they got into the pickup. He looked cheerful and relaxed, and she was tempted to grab hold of his arm, shake it and demand to know what the little scene in the restaurant had been about. Surely he would make some kind of explanation.

They stopped at the tractor dealer's, and she stood by while he explained Whit's needs and then loaded the required tractor part. Soon they were on their way again.

"Sorry about lunch being disturbed," he said cheerfully.

"I guess it was something important."

"In a way. Someone I hadn't seen in a long time."

"Really amazing that he just happened to walk into the place where we were about to have lunch."

"It didn't just happen. He'd been looking for me. The local authorities had traced me to Whit's place, and when they spotted his pickup, they knew it was a good lead."

"How methodical. He must be a really good friend to go to so much trouble."

He glanced at her, she thought, as though trying to read her mind. For a minute, she felt he was about to say something important and hoped he was going to tell her about the trouble he was in. Surely he knew she cared about him and would want to help.

He shook his head. "I've been worried about Sylvia and the girls."

The sudden change of subject gave her a little mental jolt. "You mean because of the cotton chopping being finished?"

"That and other things. Sylvia has been confiding in me a little while we work."

"I've seen the two of you with your heads together."

"She needs help, and apparently the bad feelings between her and her family are irresoluble."

"Poor Sylvia, a smashed marriage and no real family either. Couldn't she give them another chance?"

"If you're talking about her family, I don't think so. She was abused as a child, and I suppose that's one reason she married at such an early age, just to get away from home."

"From the frying pan into the fire?" Cath asked, relying on the cliché to aid her numbed brain. She was truly concerned about Sylvia and her daughters, and yet right now it was hard to think about anyone other than Douglas.

"I'm not so sure about that. After listening to her talk about her husband, I figure he's not such a bad guy."

"He abandoned them!"

"Not exactly. Apparently he and Sylvia had a big fight, and she ran off from the town where they were living, about thirty miles from here."

"What town?"

"Place called Clinton."

"That's not far. He could find her if he wanted to."

"Sylvia hasn't gone looking for him. They're both proud; they haven't learned the skills of compromise. It's a shame that a marriage has to fall apart because a couple of adults are acting like children. It's rough on those two little girls."

"Marriages seem to fall apart easily these days," Cath said, thinking of Whit and Angie. "People don't hang on the way they used to."

He nodded. "It's not easy. Things go wrong, and even people who care about each other are torn apart. Obviously, Whit didn't want the divorce, but he doesn't seem to be able to stop it. I feel sure that when he married he fully intended to make a commitment for life."

Something in his tone almost made her shiver. "If I ever marry, I'll feel that way. I'll do everything I can to make it work."

"If you marry?" His tone was teasing now. "A pretty girl like you?"

She regarded him seriously. "I have some rather definite plans for my life. It'd take just the right man to share it with me."

"I'm sure God has someone in mind for you," he said, his tone still light, so that she couldn't help wondering if he was making fun of her. "Now the lucky man only has to get you to agree."

She turned furiously away from him. "I wish you wouldn't tease. I've never been more serious about anything in my life."

"Nor have I," he said. They were out in the country now, and in a reenactment of an event earlier in the day, he steered the pickup over onto the grassy shoulder of the road. This time the expanse was wide enough to put them out of the flow of traffic, but privacy was nonexistent as a fast-moving truck whizzed by. He reached over to pull her into his arms.

Her mind whirled and circled dizzily, like a helicopter searching the landscape below. Confusing, contradicting thoughts swarmed in profusion through her head. She loved him, but how could she? He wasn't a man she could respect. A shady past. But no, it couldn't be. He wasn't like that. Besides, people changed. But did they really? Perhaps he was only a particularly talented con artist.

They kissed, and for that moment all thought was banished, and she reacted out of instinct and emotion, feeling, not thinking. He smelled good, fresh and outdoorsy, like a man who worked in the open. His lips were strong and possessive, demanding. From somewhere in the distance, she heard the roar of another approaching vehicle. A minute or so later, she looked up in time to see it hurry past.

She pulled away. "Everyone in the county will see us this time."

"I don't care." His voice was husky and he reached for her again.

She moved to the extreme edge of the seat. "I do. Anyway, it's time we got home."

She couldn't bear the hurt look that came into his eyes. "Gran will be worried about us," she explained hurriedly.

"She thinks you're out with Whit. She won't be worried. She trusts him."

She didn't look up to meet his eyes. "I'm concerned about her. I need to get home."

"She's not alone. Sylvia and the girls are there. Besides, she seems much improved."

"She's practically well. I'll be able to go home soon."

"Cathleen." He reached for her hand, holding it in both of his. "I can tell you're not ready to listen now, but promise me you won't go running off home without telling me. I've got to talk to you first."

She didn't respond. She was too miserable to make any promises, and after a few moments of silence, he started the engine and drove on again. When she stole a quick glance at him, she saw his face looking white and set.

When they got to the farm, she left him and Roberto to unload the groceries and hurried inside, rushing past her grandmother, who came to the door to greet her.

"Where's the fire?" her grandmother called irritably after her. "Can't you even stop and chat for a second?"

"Sorry, Gran, I'm a little tired," Cath called, not wanting to stop for fear she would break into tears like a little child. She hurried to her room, closed the door behind her and flung herself on the bed. But the tears didn't come.

She rolled over and stared at the ceiling, thinking how foolish she'd been. Why hadn't she just asked him about it? Doubtless there was some good explanation for his behavior.

But what explanations could be adequate to explain the reappearance of Gran's little jewelry box just after she'd seen him slipping away from the house? Or to make her understand why the local police had come looking for him today? She wanted to believe in him. Underneath everything she did believe. But that didn't resolve their differences. As sincerely as she believed anything in life, she was convinced that she would be a very unhappy person if she allowed her life to drift meaninglessly. She had to feel that she was spending her days usefully, doing more than earning a living. It was disconcerting to think what might happen to her aspirations if she gave way to her feelings for Douglas Boyd. She'd had everything so neatly mapped out, and now he was upsetting all the carefully worked out details. He just didn't fit into her plans, that was all.

A sharp rap sounded at her bedroom door. "Cathleen, I have to talk to you."

Cath sat up, brushing her hair back into place. "Come in, Gran."

Her grandmother opened the door and entered cautiously, as though not sure what to expect. "I've got it all worked out," she said.

Cathleen raised questioning eyebrows. "Got what worked out?"

"They called today from the hospital."

"The hospital," Cathleen repeated in a whisper. "Oh, but Gran..."

"You could have told me." Gran sat on the bed. "Did you think I wanted you to give up something important like that just to look after me?"

"Oh, Gran." Cathleen stretched out a hand. "You're important, too. I wanted to be with you."

"But you wanted to be in Mexico, too, child. Don't you think I can understand what an opportunity this is to get wonderful experience and help people really in need at the same time? And you haven't mentioned a word of it to any of your family."

Cathleen swallowed, the tears that had been evading her all day coming to her eyes. "It's okay, Gran."

"Now it is. They called to say they had another opening on the team because one of the nurses got sick and they need help in a hurry. Thought maybe your family situation had changed and I told them it had."

"But, Gran—"

"It has changed. I'm well again, Cath."

"You're a lot better, but you still need to be careful."

"I need someone to help around the place and do things for me that I used to do myself. I may be stubborn, but I can see that. That's why I've asked Sylvia and the girls to move into the house. She's agreed to take over here for room and board and a small salary."

"But, Gran, where will you put them?"

Mrs. Price looked around the comfortable bedroom with a complacent air. "We're going to clean out the storeroom for the girls. It used to be a bedroom back when our children were small, you know. And Sylvia's coming in here."

Cathleen couldn't help laughing. "Throwing me out, are you?"

"Course I am. You're heading for Mexico. They want you there as soon as possible. You'd better get up from that bed and start packing instead of sitting there wasting time."

She threw her arms around her grandmother's neck, hugging her fiercely. "Oh, Gran, you're quite a lady."

"You'd better believe it. If I was ten years younger, I'd be going to Mexico with you. But as things stand, I'm glad to have Sylvia and the girls for company. It's too bad Whit hasn't been as lucky."

"What do you mean?"

"Roberto told him this afternoon that he's got to head home. Seems he's got a girl he can't wait a minute longer to see. Besides, he's got some work to do on his family's place before he starts college this fall."

Cathleen's mouth went dry. "But he'll still have Douglas."

Gran frowned thoughtfully. "Apparently not. Roberto said he felt sure Douglas would be leaving, too. Said his time was about up and he'd be going back to his real life."

"Time?" Cathleen asked in total confusion.

Gran shrugged. "Don't ask me to explain, but it sounds as though they'll both be moving on. Men like that don't stick around long as a rule."

"I suppose not." Cathleen felt numb. It was over. She'd made her choice, the only one she could make. Douglas Boyd was basically a fine man; she was convinced of that in spite of appearances to the contrary. But he could have no part in her life.

"Anyway, the one for you to worry about is Whit. He got some sort of word from Angie today, and he's really down in the mouth."

"You know he didn't take me into town?"

Gran nodded. "He came by after you left. Said he felt so bad that he knew he wouldn't be good company, but after you left he figured out that the one thing he really needed was to talk to you. I promised to send you over."

"He's really upset?"

"Worse than I've ever seen."

"Then I'd better go over there right now." Cathleen got to her feet.

"You'd better hurry. I told those folks from the hospital that you'd be in Oklahoma City first thing in the morning."

"In the morning!" Cath gasped.

Gran nodded as though proud of herself for arranging the whole thing. "I've already taken care of everything. There's a bus leaving town at eleven, and you can ask Whit to drive you up. While you're over talking to him, I'll get Sylvia to get your things together."

Cath continued to stare at her grandmother. "You've really got everything all planned out."

"It's in my nature. I'm the executive type. Now get going."

Cath hurried out of the house and out to Gran's car, still feeling a little as though she were operating on automatic. It was finally happening, and the dream of her life was about to come true. But first, Whit! They'd been friends for such a long time, and she had to do what she could to help him through these bleak moments.

She found him in the big hay barn out back of his house, gazing down at the floor. The sweet smell of hay made her sneeze. "Gran sent me looking for you."

"I wanted to talk to you." He regarded her soberly. "About something important."

She waited, not knowing what to say.

"Guess in spite of everything I kept hoping it'd work out."

"You're talking about Angie?"

He nodded. "You know how I feel about her, and I thought she felt the same. I just knew we'd get back together."

"It could still happen." Her voice was gentle.

He shook his head, pain visible in his face. "I sat around and waited, figuring some magic would happen, I suppose. And in the meantime, things were rolling on. People who really care about each other can just miss each other in passing because the right words are not said, or one or the other is afraid to apologize. I finally called her today, Cath, and I found out she married someone else day before yesterday."

"Married! I didn't even know you were divorced yet."

"Hasn't been long. She didn't waste much time."

Cath closed her eyes, overwhelmed by the tragedy of it all. It was easy enough to guess what had happened. Poor, impulsive little Angie had probably rushed into marriage just to show Whit. And now they—and maybe her new husband—would pay for that rash action for the rest of their lives.

"Guess it was my fault. Should have gone to her and told her I loved her, and that the way I felt mattered more than anything, even this farm."

It didn't do any good to agree. He was already hurting enough. "I'm sorry, Whit," was all she could say.

He straightened his sagging shoulders. "It's water under the bridge now, Cath. That's why I wanted to talk to you. I want to ask you to marry me."

In spite of her grandmother's hints, she was stunned. How could he tell her in one minute that he was still in love with his wife and in the next ask her to marry him?

"That's crazy, Whit."

His grin was crooked, and his eyes looked like those of a sick puppy. "Why not? We like each other and we've always gotten along real good. You aren't even put off by farm life the way Angie was."

She had to say it in such a way that the question would never come up again or otherwise their friendship would be destroyed. "You're not in love with me, Whit. Don't you think I deserve a chance to have somebody care about me the way you do for Angie?"

He drew in a deep breath, and she knew she'd touched the right chord. "You're in love with Doug."

She hated the thought that her feelings were that obvious, but she would use even that to prevent what was happening in his mind.

"I'm in love with him, as much good it does me. I'm leaving tonight, Whit, and going to Mexico to take a temporary apprentice assignment with a medical team from the hospital where I work. It's a big step for me, getting this chance."

She thought he would approve. No doubt he was like Gran and convinced that her attachment to Douglas Boyd was a dangerous one.

He grinned, looking almost like his old self. "Don't run away from it, Cath. Take it from someone who knows."

She wouldn't debate the point. "I've got to catch a bus at eleven tonight. Will you drive me into town?"

He studied her face, then finally nodded: "If you're sure that's what you want."

Chapter Twelve

Back at the house, Cath found most of her packing already done. Sylvia had heated soup and made sandwiches, and Gran insisted that Cath sit down and eat whether she was hungry or not.

The toasted cheese sandwiches were more than she could manage, but the chicken vegetable soup went down easily enough. She watched Sylvia scurry around, putting the last of her things into a suitcase.

"Are you really leaving, Cath?" Mary Ann put down her soupspoon to ask.

"Afraid so, honey."

"If you're afraid, then I don't think you should go."

Cath's laughter sounded a little weak. "I didn't really mean I was afraid, Mary Ann. I'm pleased to get the chance to do this work. It's just that at the same time I'm sorry to leave you all behind."

Kristina banged emphatically on the table with her spoon, and her older sister reached over to restrain her. "No, Kristina." She frowned, then turned her attention back to Cathleen. "But you'll come back."

"I promise I'll come back. And I'm so glad that you and Kristina and your mom will be with Gran while I'm away. It makes me feel so much better just knowing you'll be here."

The little girl seemed comforted by the words and went back to eating, but her mother was agitated. Her face was flushed a deep red. "Mrs. Price, Cathleen, I want to talk to you."

"Well, talk then," Gran ordered.

"I need to talk to you privately." Sylvia looked at her daughters. "Perhaps we could go back into one of the bedrooms."

"You can talk here," Mary Ann said, sounding virtuous. "I won't listen."

"I don't want to interrupt your supper," her mother said firmly. "Besides, this is not your concern." Her eyes looked pleadingly at Cath.

She got to her feet. What was going on now? Sylvia seemed quite upset. "Let's go back to my room. That way I can check to make sure I've got everything while we talk."

Cath led the way, with Sylvia and Gran following. Back in the bedroom, Gran sat down on the bed, looking expectantly at Sylvia. Cath went over to peer into the nearly empty closet, trying to make the focus a little less intense. "Looks like you packed everything, Sylvia."

Even though the dark-haired young woman stood still, Cath had a feeling of hand-wringing. Sylvia was almost visibly nervous, though only her large dark eyes showed that emotion.

"You've been so kind to me. I had to tell you."

"Tell us what, Sylvia? Quit hemming around and just come out and say it."

Cath smiled at her grandmother. "Give her a chance, Gran, she's trying."

"It's hard. But I can't let you take us in here, give us a new start, without telling you the truth. I just want you to know that I never did anything like that in my life before."

Gran bounced indignantly on the bed. "Did what?"

Sylvia bit at her lower lip, still hesitating. "I was angry and upset and a little out of my head, I guess. That's why I took it."

"Took what?" Cath frowned.

"It was when we came here, the very first day." Sylvia looked at Cath, rather than at her grandmother, as though the trusting gaze of Mrs. Price was more than she could bear. "Your grandmother brought us into the house to find some blankets and things for us to use. I opened the drawer in her dresser and found her jewel case. I took it."

Cath felt as though she'd been struck by lightning, as though thunder roared around her. "You took it? But I saw..."

"Then I didn't just put it in the wrong drawer!" Gran interrupted triumphantly. "That's a load off my mind."

Sylvia put trembling hands up to her face. "I know you'll want me to go away now that you know I'm a thief."

"Nonsense." Mrs. Price glared at her. "You brought it back, didn't you? Proves you don't have it in you to steal. Besides, it's hard for me to know what I might do if I had babies going hungry, isn't that right, Cath?"

Still stunned, Cath nodded.

"But I didn't bring it back. Douglas did. I went to him for help and told him what I'd done. Somehow, I wasn't afraid of him like I was of everybody else. And he put it back and said it would be like it had never happened." She stared defiantly at them. "But I couldn't feel right until I told you, too."

Gran got up, brushing wrinkles from her dress. "Well, you've told us, so now you'd better get back in there and see what those two rascals are up to. With my children, I learned quick enough that when things got too quiet, trouble was brewing."

Sylvia stared at her. "You mean you don't want me to go away?"

"Not likely to cut my nose off to spite my face. I need you here, Sylvia. Besides, I like your company and those two little girls."

A kind of incredulous joy filled Sylvia. "It's going to be perfect," she whispered. "If only Eric were here to see how well things are working out for us."

"If you feel that way, why don't you contact him and ask him to come back?" Cath asked impulsively.

The joy faded. "Douglas found out where he'd been living, and I wrote to him and told him I was sorry for the quarrel and everything, and that we missed him. Douglas wrote, too. But we didn't get any answer, so I guess it's really over and he doesn't want us back."

Gran patted her shoulder. "You never can tell about men, my dear; they do the oddest things sometimes. But if we can find him, we'll just put him to work for Whit until he can find something that pays better. And Whit and me both, we've got a few friends in this community, so I'm sure that wouldn't take too long."

Tears filled Sylvia's dark eyes. "If only it could happen that way. It was because he couldn't get work that he was so unhappy and mad all the time. It made him feel like he'd failed us."

"Sounds like you've been doing some growing up, Sylvia," Gran said, commending her. "I reckon your marriage stands a lot better chance when you get back together."

"If we get back together." Sylvia sounded hopeless.

Mrs. Price refused to tolerate such a defeatist attitude and shooed her back to the kitchen, stopping only to give Cath orders. "It's getting late, so you'd better get your bath and dress. Whit will be by for you before long now."

Cathleen obeyed, lingering a little over a hot bubble bath, but dressing quickly enough afterward, putting on her light-blue suit while checking the clock, which showed that time was moving quickly toward ten-thirty. Just enough time to get into town, buy her ticket and catch the bus.

"Whit's here!" Gran called, knocking on her bedroom door.

"Be right there." Cathleen couldn't help dreading the next few moments. The adventure ahead was an exciting one, and she'd looked forward to it for so many years, but goodbyes were always hard and this one was going to be particularly difficult.

Kristina had fallen asleep, but Mary Ann was as wide awake as the adults and submitted patiently to the hug Cath gave her. Cath couldn't refrain from hugging Sylvia, too, feeling closer to her after the night's revelations. "Take care of Granny for me."

"Granny my foot!" Gran gave her a whack with one hand as though she were as young as Mary Ann. "'Granny' was my grandmother; I prefer to be called Gran."

Cathleen grinned, but felt tears come to her eyes as she put her arms around the slender, elderly woman. "Take care, darling Gran."

Gran hugged her fiercely but didn't speak a word, and Cath felt Whit's strong hand steering her from the house. Blinking back tears, she ran across the yard with him to climb into Gran's little car. "Your grandmother said we should go in style tonight," he told her, "so we're leaving my pickup at home."

Cathleen tried to smile, but looked around a little wildly as a feeling of desperation began to well up inside her. She couldn't go away like this.

"Where are Roberto and Douglas? I wanted to say goodbye to them."

"Oh, they've been gone all evening. Some guy came by, said he wanted to talk to them and they went off with him." He stared at her, still not starting the car. "Cath, I don't think you should leave without talking to Doug, considering the way you feel."

She gulped back tears. "It wouldn't make any difference. The feelings are all on my side."

"Look, hon, I'm not sure of that at all."

She smiled through her tears at him. It was good to have her old friend back. "Just tell them both I'm sorry I didn't get to say goodbye. No, tell Roberto *adios* and thanks for the Spanish lessons."

"And Douglas?"

"Just goodbye."

He started the car and Cathleen waved at Sylvia, who was standing on the little back porch as they drove down the road into the darkness.

They were halfway to town before she was in enough control of herself to speak again. "Wonder who the man was who wanted to talk to Roberto and Douglas."

"Older guy with gray hair. Kind of distinguished-looking."

Cath digested this. "It must have been the same man who came into the restaurant today to talk to him. He sure is persistent."

For several miles Whit seemed to be considering something. "Doug called him 'Dad.'"

Cath turned to him in disbelief. "His father?"

"Seems like."

She shook her head. "He's such a puzzle. I'll never figure it out. If you ever find out the true story about him, write to me in Mexico and let me know, will you?"

The lights of town shone just ahead. "And you're going to let it end like that?"

She didn't even want to think about it because it was too painful. "I don't have much choice."

He didn't make another attempt to argue with her until after they'd bought her ticket and she was waiting for sight of the bus that would make only a brief stop, just long enough for her and two other passengers to board.

"Cath, sometimes people can miss each other only by a little bit and it can last for the rest of their lives."

She touched his hand. "I'm sorry about you and Angie, Whit."

His face hardened. "I wasn't talking about us. I don't know what the story about Doug is, but I've worked in the fields beside him. I know how he thinks and feels about things, and I can tell you he's a fine man."

The bus had pulled into place and the other two passengers had already boarded. "Come on, miss," the driver called.

She grabbed at Whit's hand. "It isn't him," she tried to explain. "It's me. It's the two of us together." She reached up to place a quick kiss on the side of his face. "Thanks for everything, Whit." She ran to get on the bus, taking an isolated seat near the back.

As the bus pulled out, she could see the big man still standing silently beside the road, staring after it. "Oh, Whit," she said, wondering why she couldn't have fallen in love with someone safe like him. But he loved Angie and she loved Douglas, and those were the facts with which they both would have to live.

For the first few miles she tried not to think at all, but after a little while she tried to concentrate on her future. After a wasted summer, she was about to make full use of her life. She should be glad, instead of feeling so miserable.

By the time the bus stopped at the next town to pick up a few more passengers, she was giving herself a little pep talk. Life isn't so bad, she tried to tell herself. But it was hard to believe.

When one of the passengers, a thin, youngish-looking man in shabby clothing, found his way back to sit next to her, she couldn't help resenting the loss of privacy. She'd needed time alone to think things through. Nothing seemed to be working out tonight.

"Hi," he said, smiling at her. "You just get on here at Clinton?"

She shook her head. "I boarded at the last stop."

She closed her eyes, leaning back against the seat as though too tired for conversation. It seemed a reasonable excuse to avoid contact since it was getting late into the night.

A wasted summer! The thought came back to her and the events of the past few weeks replayed themselves in her mind. She'd come to Western Oklahoma resentful about missing her opportunity to go to Mexico, but she had to recognize that any time spent with the wise old woman who was her grandmother could never be entirely wasted.

Besides, she'd gotten started with her Spanish after all, thanks to Roberto. She couldn't help smiling at the thought of him. She was glad he was going to get his chance to go to school and be with his girl again. He knew what counted in his life. He would never run away from his feelings.

But I'm not running away! She came close to saying the words out loud and, glancing at her companion, was glad she hadn't. He looked her way with a frown.

"You okay?"

"Sure, I'm fine." She tried to settle down again. It had been a funny summer. Douglas and Roberto had come, and then Sylvia and the girls. People of one kind or another in need.

She'd learned to reach out in individual ways to try to meet those needs. Never again would she look at the poor and hungry as a mass crowd of unfortunates; she would see the person behind the need.

No, it hadn't been a wasted summer. She would be a better nurse for the experiences of the past few weeks. She smiled. Why was she so surprised? Circumstances had sent her here when all her plans had been for Mexico and a chance at a new direction for her career. Life seemed to have its own rhythm, its own time for things to happen, and now she was finally going to Mexico.

And didn't want to go!

"Are you sure you're all right?"

She turned to the young man in the next seat. "I'm fine. Why do you ask?"

"You keep looking out the window and you have a funny look on your face."

"I'm just sorry to be leaving my friends behind."

He sighed, looking weary and sad. "I'm leaving people behind, too, only it's my family."

"That's too bad."

He nodded. "But they'll be better off without me. Sylvia's got things going her way now. She doesn't need me."

Cathleen stared at him. She swallowed hard. "You got on at Clinton," she said, as though it was an accusation.

He nodded, frowning in a puzzled way. "I told you that."

"I know a Sylvia. She has two little girls."

He paled, but met her gaze steadily. "We have two little girls, Mary Ann and Kristina."

She nodded, but couldn't say anything.

He reached for her, though he didn't actually touch her but his clutching hand kept grasping air. "Are they all right?"

"I just left them a little over an hour ago. They're fine."

He seemed to sink into his seat. "I knew they'd be better off without me."

"But they need you. How can you go off without them? Mary Ann expected you back for her birthday."

He didn't look to be much older than Sylvia, but now his face seemed to age before her eyes, lines of worry deeply etched in it. "I was sick and couldn't get work. Sylvia told me I was a failure and she was right. How could I go to them?"

"But they want you, no matter what. Sylvia's sorry for the things she said."

He shook his head. "I got a letter from her and from her friend, too. They both said I should come back. But they also said she and the girls were all right. She's looked after them better than I could, so how can I go back now?"

"So you're just running away?"

"Not that. There's more work up at Oklahoma City than out here. I'm going to get a job and save some money. Then when I go back they'll be proud of me."

Cathleen wanted to argue, wishing she could somehow turn the bus around so that it headed back west and toward the farm. Didn't he see that he was making a mistake and that they wanted him back right now, no matter what?

"The friend of Sylvia's who wrote, was his name Douglas Boyd?"

He nodded. "That's right. Seemed real down to earth for a minister. You know, in touch with things."

She couldn't help smiling. "Douglas isn't exactly a minister," she said.

He frowned. "Funny, I got that impression, but no matter what, I could tell he was the kind of man who understood people's feelings and the things that really matter. If Sylvia and I had managed to talk to each other, had kept in touch with how we were each feeling inside, I feel we wouldn't have come apart the way we did."

Cathleen leaned back, staring out into the blackness. It was very late now and the night seemed to have a nightmarish quality. She tried to think, but the logical, reasoning part of her brain seemed to be on hold. She could only feel.

What had she done? Leaving like this tonight had been only a kind of panicked flight from the complications caused by her emotions, so that she was not so much rushing toward something as escaping.

"Yep, he sounded like a really fine man, this Doug Boyd," Sylvia's husband said.

She closed her eyes. He'd known from one letter what it had taken her all summer to learn. What a snob she'd been! She'd had to have the facts painted in bold colors. Douglas Boyd was a man of character, who could reach out to others with a unique sensitivity. What did it matter if he labored as an unskilled farm worker? What did anything matter but that she loved him?

She blinked back tears, staring out into the blank wall of darkness. It was late. The only other traffic on the road was the trucks that roared past them. As soon as they got to Oklahoma City, she would purchase her return ticket and go back west to find him.

But what if he'd already gone? What if he'd vanished as easily as he'd come into her life? She might never find him again.

"I sure miss saying good-night to my little girls," Eric Marlowe said.

She glared indignantly at him. "Then I don't see why you're running away."

He sank back without retorting, and she couldn't help thinking that she didn't have a right to criticize. She was doing the same thing—running away.

Abruptly the big bus lurched, and she was thrown against the side as it moved over onto the shoulder. Sleeping passengers were startled to wakefulness and she heard surprised comments from all around.

"Nothing to be concerned about, folks," the driver called. "Just a slight problem."

Most of the passengers settled down, either going back to sleep or talking in low tones. Then the driver opened the door and got out.

"I've had some experience repairing cars," Eric Marlowe told her. "Maybe I'd better get out and see if I can help."

Cathleen followed him, though more to see what was going on than because she expected to be of any real assistance. Outside, they found the driver staring at a very flat tire.

"Brand-new tires," he told them. "Just had them put on at Amarillo. Can't understand it."

"Doesn't seem to be a very serious problem," she told him.

"Nope, just a minor delay. But we're all tired and anxious to get into the city."

Cathleen stared around into the darkness of the country night. Another truck whizzed past, and then a second vehicle approached, slowing as it came up to them, then pulling up behind the bus.

"Having trouble?" a familiar voice called.

Douglas! Cathleen froze for a moment, then she ran toward him.

"Cathleen!" He held out his arms and she ran straight into his embrace.

"I thought I'd never see you again," she said, sobbing against his chest.

"You don't think I'd let you get away that easily? When Whit told me you'd gone, I headed right out after you. I told him he'd get his pickup back someday, but I had to find you first. I cut across country to intersect you at the Clinton stop, but the bus had just pulled out. I've been chasing after you ever since."

"I was coming back, but I was so afraid I'd miss you."

He hugged her tighter. "I love you, Cathleen. Did I get a chance to tell you that yet?"

"I knew it already," she said in a meek little voice. "I love you, too. And we'll work out our differences."

He pushed her gently away to hold at at arm's length, studying her face by the light cast from the pickup. "I don't think that's going to be too hard, my love, because I firmly believe that the two of us were meant to live and work together."

Suddenly Cath was aware they had an audience of not only Eric and the bus driver, but several interested passengers who were peering through the windows. She took his hand in hers and led him toward the two men.

"This is Sylvia's husband," she said, "the one you wrote to. He thinks you're a minister."

The two men shook hands. "I am a minister," Douglas said, "but it's taken me the last few weeks to find out for sure that I'd chosen the right profession." He looked at the driver. "Something we can do to help?"

The driver shook his head. "Just a matter of fixing a flat," he said, sounding disgusted. "And what I can't get over is that these are brand-new tires. Only had them put on in Amarillo."

Cath squeezed Douglas's hand. She didn't understand a lot of what was happening, but she knew with a rising certainty that it was all right, anyway. Somehow she and Douglas had come together and now the two of them could work out all their problems. She wondered how he'd feel about spending the rest of the summer in Mexico.

"We'll have to take Eric back to the farm with us," she told him, then reached up to kiss him, not even caring that a whole crowd of people looked on. "I can't wait to see Sylvia's face when she sees him."

Douglas smiled down at her, then leaned close to whisper. "I didn't know a flat tire could be a miracle."

You won't want to miss a single one of the heart-felt stories presented by Silhouette Special Edition; and when you take advantage of this special offer, you won't have to.

You'll also receive a FREE subscription to the Silhouette Books Newsletter as long as you remain a member. Each lively issue is filled with news on upcoming titles, interviews with your favorite authors, even their favorite recipes.

To become a home subscriber and receive your first 4 books FREE, fill out and mail the coupon today!

Silhouette Special Edition®

Silhouette Books, 120 Brighton Rd., P.O. Box 5084, Clifton, NJ 07015-5084

Silhouette Special Edition

AMERICAN TRIBUTE

RIGHT BEHIND THE RAIN
Elaine Camp #301—April 1986
The difficulty of coping with her brother's
death brought reporter Raleigh Torrence
to the office of Evan Younger, a police
psychologist. He helped her to deal with
her feelings and emotions, including love.

CHEROKEE FIRE
Gena Dalton #307—May 1986
It was Sabrina Dante's silver spoon that
Cherokee cowboy Jarod Redfeather couldn't
trust. The two lovers came from opposite
worlds, but Jarod's Indian heritage taught
them to overcome their differences.

NOBODY'S FOOL
Renee Roszel #313—June 1986
Everyone bet that Martin Dante and Cara
Torrence would get together. But Martin
wasn't putting any money down, and Cara
was out to prove that she was nobody's fool.

MISTY MORNINGS, MAGIC NIGHTS
Ada Steward #319—July 1986
The last thing Carole Stockton wanted was to
fall in love with another politician, especially
Donnelly Wakefield. But under a blanket of
secrecy, far from the campaign spotlights,
their love became a powerful force.

Silhouette Romance

COMING NEXT MONTH

THE INFAMOUS MADAM X—Joan Smith
Winning the auto show became a slim possibility when Brett
plowed into "Madam X"—Mila's antique Cadillac. She was
angry at first, but like the roar of a powerful engine, the heat of
passion eventually exploded.

LOOKALIKE LOVE—Nancy John
Cleo agreed to model for a new advertising campaign because she
was an exact lookalike of the original model. She didn't know
charading as Kent's girlfriend was part of the contract.

IRISH EYES—Lynnette Morland
Roberta was on the brink of superstardom, until Irish chauvinist
Christy O'Laighleis arrived. He claimed she was the American
enemy sent to export Irish talent—and he would do anything to
stop her!

DARLING DETECTIVE—Karen Young
Sidney was an ace financial detective. But Beau didn't think
women and business mixed. While unmuddling his finances,
maybe she could also teach him a thing or two about the business
of love.

TALL, DARK AND HANDSOME—Glenda Sands
They were too different—the playboy and the prude. Juliet's
values and life-style could never blend with Morgan Jay
Stanton's. But it's not always easy to resist such sweet temptation.

STOLEN PROMISE—Christine Flynn
Was Britt really innocent of involvement with the art thefts?
Creed wanted to believe her, despite the evidence against her. He
didn't put her behind bars, but her heart was being held captive.

AVAILABLE THIS MONTH: